# Many Faces
# to
# Many Places

a story

## Judy Azar LeBlanc

*Many Faces to Many Places*
by Judy Azar LeBlanc

Printed in the United States of America

ISBN 1-594678-66-9

www.xulonpress.com

Nov 14, 2006

To Steven ~

With Love

Judy Ann LeBlanc

# Contents

*Prologue* ................................................................ vii

**Part I** ..........................................................................**9**
   Flight in the Night ................................................ 11
   The Land of Many Trees .................................... 25
   Mount Splendor .................................................. 35
   The Meadow ........................................................ 45

**Part II** ......................................................................**49**
   The Land of Forgotten .......................................... 51
   The Lost Kingdom ................................................ 63

**Part III** ....................................................................**73**
   The Ascent ............................................................ 75

*Epilogue* .................................................................. 91

# Prologue

M any Faces to Many Places is a story of the adventurous
journey of a courageous spirit who, in search for freedom,
travels through the world of timeless knowledge. It is an allegory that
depicts a process we may all go through as we grow in understanding
and knowledge in setting out to establish a path of our own.

# Part I

# Flight in the Night

Many Faces stared at the full moon through the window. She wondered if it knew how her heart ached to taste freedom. For too long she had been locked in a one-room cabin tucked in the middle of the woods. She tried to flee, but the mean, old, cross-eyed witch with a big wart on the tip of her nose always caught her, brought her back, and locked her in a closet for days.

Many Faces knew that someday the witch would forget to hide the key. She had to. And when that day came, Many Faces planned to make a fast run for it. That is where her faith and hope rested.

Then a strange thing happened. The moon lowered itself down to the window, lit the cabin and whispered, "Now is your chance, Many Faces. Follow me, for there is something special that you must see."

That was Many Faces' cue. With the witch snoring louder than usual, and with the help of the moon's light, Many Faces knew now was the time to find the key. She looked around. There it was, right next to the small sack of leftover bread on top of the stove.

"Thank you, Mr. Moon," she whispered, quickly grabbing the key and the bread. Once outside she quietly closed the door, locking the witch in, and flung the key as hard and as far as she could.

"Ah, free at last," she sighed.

The woods could be a scary place, if one did not have the gift to communicate with all creatures as Many Faces did. The normal life of the night creatures was simple and quiet. The males left their families at home while they went out to scavenge for food. Occasionally, one could hear the screams of protest as an animal tried to cross a territory line, but that was it.

Tonight, however, the light of the moon brought out entire families, and the noise was exceptionally loud. As the males rummaged through the brush, the females visited and watched their young play hide and seek. Except for the audible words of "Come out, come out wherever you are" shouted by the offspring, the rest of the words were garbled and frightening.

Suddenly, a strong gust of wind came from the mouth of the North Wind. "Look, Many Faces," the North Wind howled. "There's nothing but the full vastness of space."

As Many Faces stared into the vast night, a burly man jumped out from behind a tree and stood before her. Dressed in inky black, his eyes were like slits. "Do not take one step forward," he yelled in a thunderous voice, pointing a silver sword at her chest.

Many Faces fell to her knees, trembling.

"Who do you think you are?" the burly man shouted. "There is nothing special out there in that great, big world waiting for you! Look for yourself! Can't you see the vast emptiness that awaits you? Turn back! Return to the witch, you ungrateful little woman. She at least gave you food and shelter."

Perhaps it was all just an illusion caused by the fear she was feeling. Nonetheless, Many Faces boldly replied. "I can't! I won't! I will never go back! That closet was emptier than you say the world out there is, and I was always alone! No," she cried, "let that sword of yours penetrate my heart, for therein lies the true emptiness that I feel, and the kind of hunger I have, no chewable food could ever satisfy."

Many Faces squeezed her eyes tight. She could taste the salt of the sweat and tears pouring down her face. The pounding of her heart grew louder. Hours seemed to pass, but nothing happened. Many Faces finally opened her eyes. The burly man was gone! Had he really been there at all? she wondered. Then she heard him say,

*"To be paralyzed in the face of fear is only temporary, but to never go beyond is crippling for life."*

Many Faces smiled when she heard the voice. To find that she had the courage to take on such a powerful enemy and triumph was a real beginning for her. It was as if she were born again. Many Faces picked up her little sack of bread and walked into the lone night to begin her journey.

Not having a care in the world made the weeks pass by quickly for Many Faces, and on one day, her spirits were particularly high. Rather than walk, she skipped and hummed a song. Suddenly, she heard the sound of flowing water. It reminded her of her hunger and thirst. She had long finished the bread, and the berries she had collected were almost gone as well.

As Many Faces stood and listened, a yellow butterfly flew up to her. "Don't worry, Many Faces, I will show you where the water is. And there is an abundance of berries there as well. You can fill up your sack again." The butterfly fluttered her wings.

"Oh, thank you. That will help a lot," replied Many Faces.

The slow running River of Time was a legend among the wildlife. Its ability to speak kept it informed and entertained by all who came by to play, swim, and refresh themselves. Although Many Faces never took her eyes off the butterfly, she knew that they were close to the water. The air smelled fresher, the shrubs greener, and the trees fuller. Then she saw it. She turned to say thank you, but the butterfly was gone. It did not matter. She would see it again. Of that, she was sure.

The peaceful sound of trickling water quieted her spirit. After quenching her thirst and nibbling on fresh berries, Many Faces stretched out and closed her eyes to take a nap. The warm rays of the sun seeped through the gaps in the trees, pierced the river, and woke it from its lazy slumber. As Many Faces drifted off, she heard a soft voice say: "Welcome, Little One of Many Faces."

"Huh? Who said that," she asked, sitting straight up and seeing no one.

"I did," said the soothing voice. "I am within the flow of the water, but you can't see me."

"Why not? Who are you?"

"I am nameless, little one. I have no beginning, and I have no end. I have always existed."

Then recognizing the voice, Many Faces replied. "Oh, I know who you are. You're called Mr. Time! What are you doing in the river? I thought you had been captured and placed in a bottle filled with sand. Why, you are so worshipped by man that they have made a golden image of you and put it in their homes. In fact, they even carry a picture of you on their wrists. How did you escape?"

"Ah, Little One of Many Faces," the voice of Time replied, "I had no need to escape, for I have never been captured. What mankind has captured is only the idea of me—created by him in his own mind. What they have seen are but the shadows left by the sun as it follows a path of its own.

"I am like the free flow of the water. I connect your past with your present, which flows on to your future. Many Faces, when you look back into those memories of time, your reflections become longings for the past that will blind you to the present and paralyze your future."

Then Time stood still and Many Faces was left alone with the gentle sound of the water. "Mr. Time," she called out, "please don't leave me yet. I need to see you. Where did you go? When can we talk again?"

"Many Faces, I didn't leave you," replied the distant voice. "I am and have always been with you, for in your spirit a thousand years is but a day. However, if you need to see me, look for me in the seasons and there you will find me."

*What words of wisdom,* thought Many Faces as she gazed out at the rippling water. It was no surprise at all when the yellow butterfly appeared on top of the ripples; wings stretched back, little legs crossed. Quite happy to be just floating down the river. *Now that looks like fun,* Many Faces thought. *Maybe she can show me how to do it as well.* She quickly jumped to her feet, grabbed her sack, and began to chase the butterfly. "Hel-lo," she called and waved.

The butterfly heard her all right, but it was not about to answer. No way, not after seeing what happened to its friends when they stopped to talk to strangers. It saw a tree, flew up to it, and hid. Fortunately, for Many Faces, the tree was on her side of the bank. "Please come down from there," Many Faces said.

"Don't come any closer to me," a voice grumped.

"Who said that?"

"I did," the tree retorted, "I am the Great Weeping Willow! Why did you wake me up, and why are you chasing my special friend, Elusive, the Great Golden Butterfly of Happiness?"

"I'm so sorry, Mr. Willow. I did not know you were sleeping. I was not going to hurt her, honestly."

"Well then, why were you chasing her?" the tree calmly asked.

"I saw her floating down the river. It looked like so much fun that I thought I would ask her if she would show me how to do it as well. I sure could use the company. Do you think you could help me talk her into it?"

"Oh, I don't think he can, Many Faces," Elusive replied, peeking down at her through the branches of the tree. "I have seen what has happened to my friends when they were lured into capture."

"What happened to them," Many Faces asked.

"Unfortunately, ruthless people hunt them down, catch them, and force them to live in cages." She sniffled. "Poor things, now that they have lost their freedom, I will never see them again. No thanks, Many Faces," she nodded, "I am not called Elusive the Great Golden Butterfly of Happiness for nothing. The more I am chased, the more elusive I become. However, I will be with you on your journey, but only in the far."

"Oh, all right, Elusive, as long as you promise me that you will stop and visit with me along the way."

"I will—only please, do call me Happiness. I prefer that name," she said as she flew back to the water.

"Thank you. I will." Many Faces waved good-bye.

"I can shelter you for the night, Many Faces," the willow offered.

"Thanks, Mr. Willow, I've just had a long rest and have to get going. But who knows, I might need to take you up on that offer some day," she replied as she walked away.

The nights turned into days and back to nights again. For Many Faces, it felt like one long and lonely night. She had not seen

Happiness since the day she left the river, not even a glimpse of her. She needed someone to talk with.

"Hap-pi-ness. Hap-pi-ness," she called. "Hap-pi-ness, where are you? You promised me that you would accompany me! You promised!"

Many Faces did not know that Happiness wanted to answer the calls, but she could not. She had made a deal with Destiny long ago that if she did not interfere with the plans of others, she could remain happy and free. She also knew that Many Faces had an important lesson to learn, so the visit would just have to wait.

"I should never have left that river," Many Faces brooded. "I will probably not see Happiness again! I should have known it was a trick! Oh, if I could only talk to her for just a few minutes, the nights wouldn't seem so long and empty and this trip wouldn't seem so lonely. I'm even starting to miss the old witch! At least I knew she was always there." Tears came to her eyes. "And what about my old friend Time. Where did he go? Oh, look for me in the seasons," she mimicked. "Why, I don't even know what season this is or how long ago that was. Oh, but how I do miss the soothing sound of his voice."

Suddenly, a strange thing began to happen. A thin line came straight out from the ground and took the shape of a human body. "Hello, Many Faces," greeted the hollow voice.

Many Faces was startled. "Where did you come from?" she asked.

"I have been with you all along, Many Faces," the voice replied, "but you have not paid one bit of attention to me."

"How can that be? I have been looking for someone to talk to for weeks! If you have really been there all along, then why haven't you appeared to me before now? Surely, I would have seen or heard you say something."

"Well, I have tried many times, Many Faces. In fact, I've been trying to talk to you for over a month now. But, you've been so busy with your self-pity, you haven't heard a word I have said to you."

"That's not true! Who are you anyway?"

"Many Faces, I don't need to tell you who I am, for you already know me. It is because of your longings for Time and Happiness that you do not see me. I have always been by your side, but you have never wanted to see me. I know the count of tears you shed when the old witch kept you behind the four walls of the dark closet. Moreover," the voice continued, "I know what you are searching for now. However, it is not my place to reveal it to you. That is something you must do on your own.

"Nevertheless, what you do need to know, Many Faces, is that it is all right for you to seek refuge in me. I will not hurt you. What is hurting you is staring back into the memories of Time. Do not forget what it said to you: '*It will blind you to the present, and paralyze your future.*'

"It is through our friendship that you will learn how to fill that emptiness. If you accept me, your knowledge will be increased and your courage will be strengthened. For the secret is not to see who you are while you are in the presence of others, but to see who you are when we are alone.

"Many Faces," the voice concluded, "to embrace me is to feel, to feel me is to know the human heart. And to know the human heart brings about understanding and compassion—both of which are very important aspects to the fulfillment of self as well as to life. Therefore, when you see me, embrace me warmly. I promise that when you do, you will feel the special embrace of life."

Many Faces cried as she listened to the voice. She knew that she could no longer keep her loneliness at bay. A choice had to be made—and now. She could either embrace it or leave it locked in the closet of Time. The only difference between now and then was that the old witch was no longer here—or was she?

The outline then floated to her, and Many Faces walked through it. "It's true. I do know who you are, Mr. Loneliness, and I have been hiding from you. I was trying so hard to convince myself that I left you back in the cabin. I thought that befriending you meant I would feel more emptiness."

"On the contrary, Many Faces, the emptiness you speak of comes from hiding those special parts of yourself from yourself. By uncovering them you will learn how to be your own best friend. This is very important to know. To have a friend, you must be a friend, and to be a friend, you must first make friends with yourself."

*What a lesson. All these years I have been running from it, and it turns out to be that simple*, Many Faces thought as she snapped her fingers. In fact, she now felt so free that she wanted to embrace it again, but it was too late. Dawn was on the horizon, and the shadow was gone. That was okay. Many Faces looked up, smiled, and embraced herself.

The sun paused on the gray horizon and took a quick peep at Many Faces. It was happy to see that she was no longer depressed and lonely. To show her how much it cared, it poured an extra amount of burnt orange and red over the horizon. Then it burst into full brightness, soared straight up, forced the night sky to change into an iridescent color of blue, and gave her a great big smile.

"Thank you," Many Faces said, clapping and smiling back.

It tickled Happiness to see them smile at each other. She fluttered her little wings at Many Faces and also smiled. Many Faces did not see the gestures, but she did catch a glimpse of the sparkle from the little wings as Happiness was leaving. "Happiness," she called and waved as she ran after her. "Happiness, please stop for a minute. It's me, Many Faces."

But this time Happiness did not see her, nor as she flew away did she hear a word Many Faces said. "Hmmm, well at least I know that she is still here with me. Perhaps she'll see me the next time."

After the long night with Loneliness, Many Faces was like new. What it said to her was true. She did feel much stronger. However, the bad habit of not stopping to eat or rest was like a thorn in her flesh, but she could not help herself. Perhaps it was because it was the first time she had ever tasted freedom, or maybe it was that she did not tire.

In either case, it made no sense. She was free as a breeze to do as she pleased. She could come, go, eat, sleep, rest, or stay where she wanted to for as long as she wanted to. No one pushed her to the point of exhaustion but herself. However, that is what she did, and now, she was so lightheaded she was about to faint. Worse yet, when she finally realized it, she was in the middle of the same valley she had seen days earlier and did not have a clue of how or when she got there. The hills she had climbed days earlier were now miles behind her.

One would think that she would at least remember the climb down. Not so with Many Faces. In her case, she felt as if she had just lost a part of her life. Then she heard a voice call out her name.

"Many Faces, Many Faces," the voice called, "come over here."

As she turned, she saw the willow waving. "Mr. Willow — it's you. What a nice surprise."

The willow was heartbroken to see that Many Faces had pushed herself to such a dangerous point. She was thin, hollow-eyed, and gaunt.

"Many Faces, you need to rest," Mr. Willow said. "Come and lie underneath my branches. I will watch over you while you sleep."

"Oh, thank you, Mr. Willow. I really do need a long rest." Many Faces collapsed, fell into a deep sleep, and dreamed.

In her dream, as Many Faces sat in the middle of a valley, a large, black bird flew in and circled her. It was about two feet long, with an extra large wing span. Although she couldn't see it very clear, it did look as though its head and neck were bald. "Is this a dream, or are you really up there?" she asked the bird.

The vulture did not answer. It couldn't. It had to be sure that Many Faces was ready to be eaten for dinner before it called in the rest of his flesh-eating buddies. Otherwise, they would make the trip for nothing, and it would end up the fool.

Suddenly, a cool and gentle breeze swept in and filled the air with a sweet scent of jasmine. "Hello Many Faces," a voice softly said as it brushed her lightly.

"Well, hello to you too," Many Faces replied to the vulture.

"I am not up there, Many Faces. Look to the west, and there you will see me."

Many Faces turned, but all she saw was a radiant light moving toward her. She was not afraid. In fact, the closer the light came, the stronger the fragrance, and the more peaceful she felt. Then the light stopped moving and formed itself into the shape of a woman. Many Faces was awed. She had not seen a miracle before now. "Who are you?" she gasped.

"Some call me the Shadow of Death while others call me by the name of Freedom," the light replied.

"Which name would you prefer that I use?"

"I cannot choose the name for you, Many Faces. That is something you must do yourself. What I can do, however, is to help you decide which one would be more appropriate for you to use. I have and always will walk beside you. I am the one who holds the key that unlocks the door for all who have been captured by their bodies. Like a bird that has been captured and is no longer able to fly, so too has mankind been captured by their birth and held hostage by the enclosure of their bodies. Mankind thinks only of living, because he is dying. But it is only in dying that he gains his freedom to live. Many Faces, it is *I* who frees them."

Many Faces was stunned by what she just heard. She had so many questions she wanted to ask the light, but the willow swept one of its long branches across her cheek and woke her up.

"Good morning, Mr. Willow. I just had the most interesting dream," she said as she yawned and stretched.

"That was not a dream," Mr. Willow replied. "You have slept for well over a week, and you sure did have us worried. In fact, your friends Time, Loneliness, and Happiness all came by to help me attend to you. Especially Happiness—she was the one who made the trips back and forth to bring you the nectar. Time brought the water, and I protected all of you while your new sweet-smelling friend stopped the vulture from calling in his buddies."

Many Faces was shocked at the news. She had no idea she had slept for so long. Moreover, she didn't know her friends cared so much about her. "Then you saw the light too?"

"Yes, I did."

"And did you hear it speak as well?" Many Faces asked.

"Yes, I did."

"Then do you know if 'it's only in dying that you gain your freedom to live' means that I'm not free because I'm still here?" she asked.

"Well, like it said, Many Faces. It is always by your side. However, what I do think is that once you have digested all that it said, you will have a much better grasp of it. What I do know for sure is that if you stay in this valley much longer, you will wither and your journey will have been for naught. You still have a lot more new friends to meet before you finish your journey, and they will guide you the rest of your way. Now that you are strong again, I suggest that you get going."

"Yes, I guess I had better. Thank you for saving my life, Mr. Willow. It seems that now I owe you one." She hugged the willow goodbye. As she turned to wave, Many Faces glimpsed the vulture turn its back and fly away. "Darn," she said, snapping her fingers. "I forgot to ask Mr. Willow about that."

The white dove kept his distance. Its instructions were to follow her to the bridge, welcome her to the new land, and then give her the good news. In that order. That was okay. The bridge was not very far, and Many Faces would reach it before nightfall. Then she saw it. The white dove took notice, quickly flew ahead, and met her at the entrance. "Welcome to The Land of Many Trees, Little One of Many Faces," greeted the dove.

"Oh, what a nice touch, thank you," she replied. "Are you one of the new friends Mr. Willow said I was soon to meet?"

"Yes, I am. I am here to congratulate you, and to give you a special gift."

"A special gift, what is it?"

"Soon you will see, Many Faces. For as you hunt for friendship, your heart searches for peace—a peace which friendship alone cannot satisfy."

"Friendship is not a means to an end, but is rather a means of giving, which is endless. Giving needs to pass freely through both of your hands, and one hand never says to the other, 'Stop, for I have already given'. When others give to you, receive it joyfully, for then you are giving and fulfilling in them that which is fulfilling in your own heart.

"Like you, each one must cross over the bridge that connects to The Land of Many Trees. Therefore, whomever you meet along the way, let it be for the sake of giving, for they are your companions and each must dream his own dream and follow his own destiny. And when you awake and find that your companion has gone, rejoice for him. Your presence here is not to stay or to possess, but rather to give and to share. By doing so you will touch the heart of another,

21

become a friend to them, and fulfill in yourself that which you seek in others."

The dove explained some of the questions that still lingered in her mind since her visit with Mr. Loneliness, but not all of them. However, by the sure wonder of its presence, a deep stillness calmed her heart and put her mind at ease. Many Faces then knew that her questions would all be answered in due time.

The dove saw the radiant look on her face and smiled. It knew it had accomplished that which it set out to do. Many Faces reached out her hand to it, and when the white dove flew up, she kissed it on the forehead. "Thank you for this gift, Mr. Dove. This new feeling is unlike anything I have ever had before. It's—well, I feel as though I am the one who is within the flow of water with my friend, Mr. Time. It feels quiescent."

"I understand it quite well, Many Faces. My gift of peace is yours to keep, and when you reach the other side, there is yet another gift waiting for you. Come, we must both leave now, for I must be in The Land of Many Trees before dark." And it fluttered its wings goodbye.

Sure enough, there it was. Who could miss it? The big gold box lay right in the middle of the road. It measured a about a foot high, a foot wide, and one and a half feet long. Except for the rounded lid, which was smooth, the rest of the box had the letters i, a, f, h, t, etched all around it. Many Faces had no idea that if she placed those letters in the correct order, they would spell the word "faith." She simply thought it was part of the design and gave them no further attention. A box such as this one, however, had to have something very valuable inside of it. At least that is what she thought. But what? She would find out. Many Faces sat down, lifted the lid slowly, and peeked inside. The moment she saw the big brown pair of eyes, she quickly slammed it back down. "Wait!" the eyes cried.

"Sooo, what am I supposed to do with these," she asked as she turned to look and see if the dove—or for that matter, anyone—was around who could answer that question for her. But there was no one, and Many Faces was too insecure to open the box again. If she did, the pair of eyes might simply fly away. She would not risk it.

She had to find out why they were there first. They had a purpose. Of that, she was sure. "Well, I assume this is the gift Mr. Dove spoke of, so I guess I'll just take it with me. I'm sure he will give me instructions later."

The gold box was heavy, and the further Many Faces carried it, the heavier it was. She would have to do something—but what? She put it down, wondering, *Is it the box that is important, the contents, or both?* She had to make a quick decision. It was tough. The pair of eyes meant something she was sure, but why were they in a gold box?

Suddenly, Many Faces heard a loud weep that touched her heart. Did it come from inside of the box? Many Faces slowly lifted the lid to see. Sure enough, the big brown eyes were crying. "Little One of Many Faces," they sniffled, "it hurts me to know that I have become such a burden to you, for I am much more precious than gold. And if you keep me in this box, I will not be able to do what I have been sent to do. Set me free, for I have been called to guide you through the new land."

"How can I do that? If I set you free and you get lost, then someone else might catch you and put you right back into a box."

"Ah, that's what is troubling you," they replied. "Well, let me put your mind at ease. I am the divine gift that was sent to you; therefore, no one else can see me but you. For those whose eyes are open cannot see as they are blinded by the lust to possess all that is around them for the sake of greed. Only when those eyes are closed can they see that which is not visible. Many Faces, I am known as the 'Eyes of Faith.' It is vital that you set me free so I may guide you, for I cannot leave this box without your permission."

"Ah, you're my Eyes of Faith! Now I understand what Mr. Willow meant when he said that new friends would guide me. What a nice gift you are," she said as she flipped open the lid and watched them soar straight out.

Eyes of Faith was both relieved and happy. Now they were free. They shot straight up into the air, blinked at her, and then smiled. "Thank you—now follow me."

It was not that easy to follow Eyes of Faith through The Land of Many Trees. Whenever Many Faces looked up, she bumped into a tree. Though Happiness was with them, she was not being very helpful. Each time Many Faces bumped into a tree, Happiness laughed at her, and each time Happiness laughed, Many Faces would look away from Eyes of Faith.

"Stop that," she scolded Happiness.

"I'm sorry, Many Faces, I can't help it. It is just that you look so funny walking with your head up in the air all of the time. Then, whack—right into a tree." She kept laughing.

"Well, it's not funny! I'm trying to follow my Eyes of Faith," Many Faces replied.

"I know, but Eyes of Faith do not expect you to follow them like that. You are supposed to watch where you are going. They'll always wait for you to catch up to them, you know."

"Why didn't they tell me so," she grumped.

"Well, now you know."

"Yes, thanks to you. By the way, Mr. Willow told me what you did for me when I was in the valley. That was very kind of you. Thank you. How come you didn't stick around?"

"I thought you already knew the answer to that, Many Faces."

"Yeah, I know, I know. They don't call you Elusive for nothing. I just wish you could stay a bit longer, that's all."

Happiness giggled. "Don't worry; we will see each other very soon. Eyes are taking you to the meadow that is on the other side of this land, and I will be there too," she said as she flew away.

*Oh, darn,* thought Many Faces as she watched Happiness leave, *I do wish she would stay longer.*

# The Land of Many Trees

M any Faces did not see the warning sign ahead of her. The dark clouds tried to tell her about the upcoming storm, but she was not watching them. She was watching the trees. She did not want to be the laughingstock of Happiness again. No sir, this time she would watch where she was going and Eyes of Faith would just have to wait. Then the sky blackened and the storm came in full force. Many Faces quickly searched the sky for Eyes, did not see them, but she did see the cave and ran for cover.

It was strange sitting alone in the dark. For a minute, Many Faces thought she heard voices in the cave and squatted to listen. *Perhaps it is Eyes, or maybe the storm that is making the noise sound like voices.*

"Eyes, is that you?" she asked. But Eyes of Faith did not answer. "He-lloo," she called out. "He-lloo—is there anyone in here?"

"We are down here," echoed a male voice. "Walk in further and wait at the rear. We will send someone to bring you down to us."

The reply thrilled her. Now she wouldn't have to wait alone. "Okaay," she yelled back. Many Faces was not sure where the back end of the cave was, and it was too dark to see where to walk, so she got on her hands and knees and felt her way until her head hit a wall. "Ouch," she moaned as she rubbed her head. "Well, at least I made it. Now all I have to do is sit and wait."

It did not take Betrayal long to find her. She knew the cave like the back of her hand. She was grumpy because she was the one who had to go and fetch her, and she did not trust strangers. Then the cavity lit up and Many Faces saw her. She was short and thin with long black hair and skin as white as snow. Many Faces stood up and waved. "I'm over here."

"I see you, I see you," Betrayal grumped. "How in the world did you get in here?"

"I crawled."

"No," she snapped. "I mean how did you find the cave?"

"Oh, that was pure luck," Many Faces replied. "I was following my Eyes of Faith through the woods when suddenly—bam! A bad storm hit. Then I lost sight of them, saw this opening, and made a run for it. I don't even know where I am at."

"Them? You mean there were others with you?"

"No, I'm alone. Eyes of Faith are the pair of flying eyes who guide me."

"Flying eyes," Betrayal winced. "I think you had better come with me, girl. It sounds to me like you need a lot more than protection from the storm. Follow me closely, and don't touch the walls! They have sharp fringes that will cut your hands, but," she added, "they will get smoother as we go down."

Many Faces had a hard time keeping up with Betrayal in the descent. It was not like being outside with Eyes of Faith who would at least wait for her. Now she had to practically run just to keep up. Betrayal did not speak or even stop for her when she fell. But that didn't matter; the torch gave enough light for her to see ahead, and now that the walls were smoother, she could use them to keep her balance.

"We are almost there," Betrayal said. "There is a short tunnel in the next wall, and once we crawl through it, we will be in the dark zone. That's where we live."

"Okay." Many Faces nodded.

Sure enough, as soon as they reached the other side, the dark zone lit up and Deception was waiting to greet her at the mouth. It had been quite some time since a stranger had been down to visit them and he was curious to see what she looked like. By cave dweller standards, Deception was the most attractive amid the men. He was hairy-faced, blue-eyed, white-skinned, wide-shouldered, and humpbacked. The news resonated through the cave. The moment

26

the dwellers heard Deception say "Welcome to the dark zone," they ran to their doors and stuck their heads out to peek at the visitor but when they saw Many Faces' slim, hairless body and vibrant skin, they quickly withdrew. "What bad taste he has," they whispered.

On the other hand, Deception had heard many stories about the light people, so he was not the least bit surprised with Many Faces' hairless face or tanned skin. "I am Deception," he announced. "You can follow me the rest of the way now."

"Thank you," Many Faces replied. "I have never been in a cave before. I had no idea they were this big."

"Be careful, she sees eyes flying through the air," Betrayal whispered in his ear.

Deception cocked his head to look at Betrayal. "Wha-aat," he whispered, staring at her in disbelief.

"Yeah, that's what she told me. Shhhh."

Now Deception was leery. Maybe it was a mistake to bring a stranger down to their dwelling. He shrugged it off. He would find out all about her soon enough.

Greedy and Stingy were just as eager to meet the stranger as their father was. The minute Many Faces walked in, they gave her the once-over. She was no threat. Stingy was shapely with pale skin like her mother, whereas Greedy was short, wide and a bit hairy like her father.

"What are you called?" Stingy blurted out.

"I am called Many Faces."

"Well, I'm Stingy and that is my ugly sister Greedy," she pointed and laughed.

Greedy turned and slapped Stingy on the arm. "Did you have to say that?" she snapped.

"Well, it's true," she slapped back. "You're fat and ugly!"

"Well, you are uglier! You look like her," Greedy snarled, pointing to Many Faces with her chin.

"Shut up," Deception shouted.

Many Faces stayed quiet. She wasn't quite sure what she was supposed to do next. The witch did not teach her anything, and she had never been with cave dwellers before. She thought it was their way of being friendly.

Deception then turned to Many Faces. "Why do they call you Many Faces?"

"I don't know," she shrugged. "That's just what the witch always called me."

"Witch!" they shrieked.

Stingy and Greedy moved closer to Betrayal and the three of them huddled. "Calm down," Deception told them. "I am sure there is a good explanation for this." He turned and eyed Many Faces sharply. He had heard a lot about the people who live in the light. They were the ones who saw things that didn't exist and then tried to convince the cave dwellers to come out and see them as well. Now, what he had to find out was if Many Faces was going to be one of them or not. "And what witch was that?"

"The one I ran away from," she answered.

"You ran away from a witch?"

"Yeah."

"How?" he asked.

"Oh, I didn't do it alone. Mr. Moon helped me."

Deception tilted his head, raised his brow, and squinted. "Mr. Moon helped you?"

"Yeah. He told me that there was something real special out there for me."

Hearing those words, they all burst out into hearty laughter. Now Deception was convinced. He didn't have to worry about having a stranger in his cave after all. Not after that wild story. Anyone who would admit to talking with the moon could not possibly be a deceiver. He would find out for sure—but later. Right now, he was too busy laughing.

"Mr. Moon told you that?" he mocked.

"And she sees eyes flying through the air too," laughed Betrayal.

Many Faces hated being laughed at, especially since she did not think there was anything funny about talking with Mr. Moon or Eyes of Faith. What would they know! They lived in a cave! Sure, it looked bigger and safer than the cabin, but it was just as dark and empty. There were no Mr. Willows, no yellow butterflies, and neither Mr. Moon nor Mr. Sun would ever find their way in to light their way or smile at them. And how would Happiness ever find them down here? She would need to be guided down too! Worse yet, how was she ever going to find her way back out? *Perhaps Eyes of Faith did not get lost in the storm and are still out there waiting for me to catch up with them,* she hoped.

"Well, Many Faces, I think that you have just found 'that special thing' right here," Deception proudly announced. "We are the famous cave dwellers. As you can see, it is nice and safe down here, the dwellings are quite comfortable, and if you join us, we will even give you your own dwelling. All you have to do is follow the simple rules of our village. However, once we do give you a dwelling, you can never leave the cave again. That is how we avoid the danger of being exposed.

"Besides," he continued, "the kind of light that is out there is too harmful. What's more, there are no witches or flying eyes down here either, only bats—and those we eat." He laughed. "Speaking of which, we need to eat. Stingy and Greedy will show you around the dwelling afterward. Then you will see for yourself why no one ever wants to leave here again."

The table was made of stone, with a thin piece of streaked calcite as a covering. The meal was a simple portion of dried seeds, roots, and bats. Many Faces had not had bats before, but after eating nothing but berries for so long, they turned out to be quite tasty. They were a bit dry and crunchy like the seeds and roots, but quite filling.

"This is the first time I have seen a place like this," Many Faces commented. "I must admit, it is a lot nicer than the cabin that I lived in."

"Thanks, it was much smaller at one time, but our neighbors, Hate and Envy, forced us to make it larger," replied Betrayal.

"As a matter of fact," Greedy added, "it was Hate who decorated the garden for us. He and Envy thought if they did, we would give it to them for extra space. But we waited for them to finish just so we could have it for ourselves." She laughed.

"Humph, yeah. They are the type that goes after your friendship only to steal whatever they can from you. What fools! They actually thought we would allow them to be our friends. Why, we would never be friends with the likes of them," contemptuously retorted Betrayal.

"Yeah, Envy just loves to copy us," Stingy added. "Each time she passes our dwelling, she peeks in to see if we have anything new and then gets one just like it. Poor thing, she wants to be like us so bad, she even went as far as naming her own brats Greedy and Stingy!"

"Gosh, do you mean to say that they are just like you?" Many Faces asked.

"How dare you say that!" snorted Betrayal. "They could never be like us! We are much better than they are!"

Deception slammed his hand hard on the table. "That's enough! I can't believe that they are still such a big part of our table talk. Many Faces, tell us more about yourself. I would much rather hear about you than about them!"

Many Faces stayed quiet a minute. What was she supposed to say now? After their last outburst of laughter, she could not say anything more about Mr. Moon, and she dared not mention Freedom, Time, Happiness, or Mr. Willow to them. So what was left? "Well," she began, "even though I never had a father like you, the witch told me that he was a very important man."

Deception squinted again. Now the question was, would he be able to believe anything else she said? "How do you know this?"

"He gave the witch this letter before he sent me away," she replied, reaching into her sack for it. "Here, I will read it to you."

> Beloved. I dare not address this letter to anyone, for when you become a woman of the world, you will understand that the rules of my life, my chosen occupation, and my other family forbade me to disclose the existence of you. My hope rests in your forgiveness. I have instructed the woman whom I have paid to care for you to be sure and tell you that I have always loved you, and each gift that I have sent to you bore the mark of my love.

"And then it's signed: 'Lovingly, your father.' "

"So, how do you know it was meant for you?" Deception asked.

"Because the witch couldn't help but remind me over and over again. And just to prove her point, she gave me it to me."

"Humph. So, where is it? Show it to us," he said.

"Where's what?"

"The gift with the mark of that strange thing he called love. Where is it?"

"I don't know. I don't have it." She shrugged. "The only thing the witch ever gave me was this letter. That's why I left. I want to find it."

"Now why would anyone want to search for something if they are not even sure that it exists?" asked Betrayal.

"But I *am* sure that it does. Otherwise, my father would not have mentioned it in his letter."

"Don't be foolish, Many Faces," Deception said. "There isn't any such thing. Everything that is out there is right here with us. Look for yourself. I am sure you can see that everything, including the thing you call love, whatever it might be, is right here with us."

True, the cave dwelling did look warm, spacious, safe, and comfortable, and it was a whole lot better than what she had known. But, still, something was missing and she could not tell what it was. "Well, nevertheless, I have to go and look for my friend, Happiness. I haven't seen her for awhile." It slipped out. Now they would want to know who Happiness was so they could laugh at her again.

"Oh, we have that too. Look, it is hanging on that wall back there," Deception pointed. "In fact, we once gave it to Envy, but after she pulled that little stunt with the garden, I sent Betrayal over to get it back for us under the guise of borrow. And when she refused, I went over and demanded that she give it back or else." His fist hit the table.

The news shocked Many Faces. But when she saw that it was only one of her look-alike friends, she simply smiled. "Ahhh, yes," she nodded.

"And there's more. We also have security," Stingy gloated.

Greedy turned to her and glared. "Shut up!" she snapped.

"Ah come on, Greedy, it's not like we're going to give her any. What harm is there in showing it off?" replied Stingy, springing up from the table. "Come on, Many Faces, I'll show you where it is."

Greedy quickly jumped to her feet. "Well, I'm going with you."

"You don't fit through the opening," Stingy scoffed.

"Well, I can keep an eye on you from the outside!"

The entry down to the secret cavity was behind a large pile of petrified wood at the back end of the alcove. Stingy and Many Faces were small enough that they did not have to move any wood to get to the opening; they simply slithered in through the side. Greedy, on the other hand, always grumbled when she had to move it. She just wished Stingy would get fat and have to move it too. This time, she had to do it fast so she could be with them when they got to the cavity, and this didn't settle well with her.

Nonetheless, by the time Stingy and Many Faces reached it, Greedy was right behind them. After Stingy crawled through, Many Faces followed. Greedy stuck her head in just to make sure things went right. Knowing the looks people gave when they first saw the treasure, she would be sure to keep a close eye on Many Faces.

But Many Faces didn't give the look. How could she? It was the first time she had ever seen these kinds of treasures. There were piles of shiny coins and carved ornaments, both dull and shiny stones, crystal cups and platters. Stacks of long, shiny bars of metal were set neatly in the corner.

Many Faces gasped. "Where did you get all of this?" she asked Stingy.

"Greedy gets it all for us."

"Oh yeah? Where from?"

"That is her secret."

"Yeah. And don't be getting any funny ideas about this, cause we know exactly how much there is here," Greedy warned.

Many Faces didn't hear a word she said, however. She was busy looking at the wonder of it all. "Gosh, if this was mine, I would sure do a lot more than just count it. Just think of what you could do with it," she said.

Stingy turned, furrowed her brows, and Greedy screeched. "I knew it! I knew it! I told you she was crazy, Stingy! And now that she has seen it, she will probably try and do exactly what Cousin Charity did!"

The reaction came as a shock to Many Faces, but not to Stingy. She was expecting it. True, Cousin Charity did have a similar idea, but she was much crazier than Many Faces, and they squelched it just fine. She just didn't see why Greedy had to be so paranoid all the time. "Gee whiz, Greedy. It's always the same with you. When are you going to learn that security means 'to look after'? Haven't we been looking after this for years?"

"Yeah."

"And have you ever seen any of us do more than count it?"

"No."

"And didn't we bury Cousin Charity under it?"

"Yeah."

"Then what is your problem?"

"She is," she twitched, pointing to Many Faces with her chin.

Many Faces turned and stared at Stingy. She wasn't sure what was going to happen next.

"Ah, I wouldn't worry about her," Stingy giggled. "You can't believe anything from a person who talks to moons and sees 'eyes' flying through the air."

Many Faces was relieved. It was a good thing she never mentioned Mr. Willow, Happiness, or Freedom to them. Freedom! She almost forgot about it. They would really think she was crazy if she told them about that! But that was okay, she knew she was quite sane.

Stingy smirked at Many Faces as she turned and crouched to crawl back out. "Come on, let's go!"

Deception was secure. He was sure that once Many Faces saw all of the security there was to have, she would stay. He relied on it. He needed more dwellers to work for Greedy. "Well, now that you've seen it, I guess you will be staying, right?"

"No, I don't think so," Many Faces shook her head. "I am pretty sure the storm is gone by now."

"What? No one who sees the kind of security we have ever leaves our cave," he shrieked.

"Ah, let her go," Stingy growled. "We don't want her here anyway. She is too ugly and she bothers us."

"Yeah. And the sooner you rid us of her, the better," Greedy added.

Deception remained thoughtful. "But what if she tells those light people about us?"

"Ahhh, I wouldn't worry about that," laughed Betrayal, shoving Many Faces out of the alcove. "She'll never make it out without a torch."

# Mount Splendor

Free at last. So what if Many Faces did not have a torch. All she had to do was crawl back through the tunnel, and if she did it coming in, then she could do it going back. But first she had to find the hole. That too should be easy. All she had to do was inch her hand over the wall as she crawled until she found it. Then, surely, once she got to the other side, Eyes of Faith would find her.

It was much easier than she thought. Once Many Faces found the hole and crawled through it, she saw a faint, twinkling light at the far end of the tunnel. It had to be Eyes of Faith. Where else could such a welcome twinkle come from? Now all she had to do was keep her eyes fixed on it. Sure enough, there they were. Bright as light. As soon as Many Faces crawled out, she saw them.

"I see you're focused again," they kidded, lighting up and winking.

"Eyes, I knew it was you! How did you know where I was?"

"That was easy. Your thoughts of me were the signal I was waiting to hear. Come on, follow me and I'll get you out of here."

The light from Eyes of Faith was much brighter than the torch light, and the cave was not as big as Many Faces thought. She was not that far down after all. Moreover, the walls did not have any of the sharp fringes Betrayal said they had; thus, she was able to use them to keep her balance going back.

Now the storm had passed and they were out. It was good to be in the light again. The air smelled fresh, the sun was bright, and Eyes glided straight up into the air. It tickled Many Faces to see them glide as free and effortless as they did. Then it hit her. There were no more trees to block her view of them. Many Faces stopped, looked back and stared. There was no path and no cave, and from where she stood, all she could see was the tree line.

"Where are we?" she asked Eyes.

"Behind you is The Land of Many Trees, and in front of you is Mount Splendor."

"But how did we get here so fast? I mean, where is the cave, the land, the path?"

Eyes of Faith winked and smiled. "It was magic."

"No, seriously, Eyes, how did we get here so fast?"

"Oh, all right. So it wasn't magic. We came out at the other end of the cave, that's all. It was a shortcut."

"But Happiness told me there was a meadow on the other side of The Land of Many Trees."

"There is, but we have to go over Mount Splendor to get there."

"Whaaat? Do we have to climb it? Why didn't Happiness tell me that?" Many Faces grumped.

Happiness would have told her, but she could not interfere with the date Many Faces had with destiny, and it was the duty of Eyes of Faith to help her with it.

"Ahhh, there you go again." Eyes said. "When are you going to learn to trust me and not Elusive? She comes and goes like the wind. Come on, let's go. Mount Splendor is not that big."

Many Faces blinked and turned. The news didn't cheer her up. She was still grumpy; nonetheless, she did as Eyes of Faith asked her to do, and headed for the mountain.

Though the path was smooth and she stayed focused on Eyes, by the time Many Faces reached the foot, she was tired, disappointed, and in no mood to climb. Now that she knew about shortcuts, she was sure there had to be one going up. But there wasn't. It was a dead end and there was no other way to get to the meadow but to climb over Mount Splendor.

"First the wilderness, then the valley, then The Land of Many Trees, then the Cave, and now this? I was expecting to be at a meadow, not cross a stupid mountain! I will never make it up there. I will die on the way up. Surely, I will just wither away and die! Maybe those cave dwellers were right after all." Many Faces sat and pouted.

Then it dawned on her, Eyes of Faith was already gone and now Many Faces had to catch them. Well, she couldn't lose sight of them. At least not now. Many Faces quickly jumped to her feet and began the climb. It was just as she thought. The brush obscured the path and Eyes were too far ahead to help her out. But that was okay. All it meant was that she scratched herself a little more than she would have otherwise.

She climbed and climbed, but still did not see Eyes. *Was it that much of a head start?* she wondered. And that is when Many Faces saw him. An old man came right out of the brush and hobbled toward her. She crouched to hide, but it was too late. The old man saw where she hid and he came straight toward her. "Many Faces, you don't need to hide from me. I am your friend," he said.

Many Faces peeked up through the brush, and when she saw that his face was marked with a thousand gentle lines, she stood. "How do you know my name?" she asked.

"I know all names," he replied. "I am the famous Old Man Pain."

"Old Man Pain! No! Go away!" she screamed. "I have heard all about you. You are not a friend at all. You are nothing but a scavenger who pounds the earth and devours those whom you will just for the sake of it!"

"Ah, such things I have heard said about me, but they are not true. I am a friend, and I always have been to those who are not afraid of me. In this case, your pain called and I came, for it is the echoing call of the need for love.

"You see, little one," he explained, "this path is the same one that love travels, and if I do not help you prepare a road for it to cross, you will not see it nor will you hear its call. I know how painful it is going to be when I break through your deep barrier, but if I do not, it will not be possible for love to reach the depth it needs for its fulfillment, and without the provision thereof, you will never know the fullness of its joy."

Many Faces had no idea that her inner pain was the call of love. It was shocking. How could something so painful be that simple? But it wasn't that simple. It was brutal. The moment she gave in to Old Man Pain, he thrust straight into her heart and ripped out the deep callus with his bare hands. Many Faces cried out in agony; then it was over. It was that brief. That is when she saw the paradox in it. The more she succumbed to him, the less she felt him. "When will I find the love you speak of, Mr. Pain?" asked Many Faces, sniffling.

"Soon. This was an essential step in your path. Now you are free to receive the love you seek, for it will be equal to all that you have suffered," he lovingly replied.

Many Faces hugged Old Man Pain and then kissed him lightly on the cheek. "Thank you. I did not mean what I said to you earlier. It is just that the things I had heard about you made me hope we would never meet. But now I'm sure glad we did."

Old Man Pain smiled and pointed with his cane. "The path to the summit is that way. If you hurry, you will reach it before nightfall."

This climb went much smoother and faster for Many Faces than it did at the onset. She looked for Eyes of Faith, but did not see them. They were at the summit with Mr. Sun, who was waiting to say good night before he disappeared. "I won't be able to wait much longer," he said to Eyes.

"Hang on. She'll be here in a minute," they replied.

Many Faces climbed over the last ridge just in time to watch the sun set. He was happy she made it in time to see him show off again. This time he would use the special effects he had with him. He lowered himself down to the walls of the cliffs, and splashed them with shades of pink, purple, green, gold, and grey. Then he dragged his shadow over them and made a collage for her to look at. Now he could say good night.

Time stood still as Many Faces watched the show in silence. She was speechless. What could she say? There were no words to describe that kind of beauty. Eyes of Faith was proud that Many Faces had so much courage. They glided over to her, blinked, smiled, and broke the silence. "Congratulations! I can tell by the look on your face that your meeting with Mr. Pain went well."

Many Faces looked up. "Thanks, Eyes. I wish I could be as happy as you are, but I am way too tired for that right now."

"That's okay. You will change your mind after you see what is next."

"You mean there is more?"

"Yes, Many Faces," a soft voice replied.

Many Faces turned to look, and saw a white rosebud next to her.

"Was that you who spoke?" she asked the rosebud.

"Yes, it was."

"I did not see you before. When did you get here?"

"I have been here quietly waiting for you to notice me, Many Faces. I am eager to share my magic with you," it softly replied. "Not only do I have the power to speak, but it was me who was in the collage that the shadow of the sun made for you.

"It is my breeze that moves the branches of trees to fan the ground below.

"It is I who changes the hues in the color of the leaves before they leave the tree, and it is I who provides the music for their dances on the ground.

"It is I who writes the songs for the birds to sing when they make their daily flights.

"It is I who paints the colors on the petals of the flowers that are seen throughout the land, and it is my perfume whose scent you smell that lies within their hearts.

"It is I who landscaped all of the gardens below the sea, and it is my crown that shines on the mountain peaks which are sometimes dressed in white.

"I provide the mist that surrounds the body of cascades as the water falls below, and it is I who provides the beat for them to follow as they seek a path of their own.

"It is I who takes your breath away when the sun bids good morning from the east and bows good night from the west.

"It is my glow you see in the moon when it exposes its fullness above the stilled waters, and it is my blanket of stars that is used to tuck you in for the night."

The rosebud was right. It was magic at its best. Many Faces watched the colored leaves dance, saw the mist around the cascades, and heard the birds say good night. Then as darkness rushed in, the moon woke up, lit the peak, and showed off its crown. And still there was more. Many Faces looked up and saw the stars form the blanket that tucked her in for the night. Then the rosebud sprayed her with perfume and whispered, *"My name is Beauty, and as you can see, the beauty that adorns the earth is not imitation."*

Happiness could not wait to see her. She had been sitting on the rosebud since dawn waiting for Many Faces to wake up. The moment she saw Many Faces stir, she flew right over, and tickled her face with her wings. "Good morning, Many Faces," she smiled as she flew back to sit on the rosebud.

"Well, good morning to you," beamed Many Faces. "What a big surprise. What are you doing here? I was not expecting to see you until I reached the meadow."

"Yes, I know. I was on my way back, but I could not resist stopping by to say congratulations to you. You've come a long way since our last visit."

"Thanks, Happiness. I've had a lot of help."

"Yes, I know. I've been watching you from afar."

"You have? Then how come you didn't stop by to say hi?"

Happiness chuckled. "Well, I'm not called Happiness for nothing you know. I have to share myself with all who follow their destiny, not just you."

"Ah, I see. Does that mean that once I reach my destiny we won't see each other again?"

"Absolutely not. What it means is that by the time you reach your destiny, you will be a lot more comfortable with my personality, that's all. Besides, by then you will have made many more friends and you won't need to be with me as much." Happiness fluttered her wings as she prepared to leave.

"I am already getting used to it," Many Faces giggled. "You have to go, right?"

"Right. But don't forget about our date."

Many Faces blew her a kiss and waved goodbye. "Oh, I won't. I am looking forward to it."

The rosebud was still sleeping. Many Faces bent down, gently kissed it goodbye, and began the descent.

It was slow. Many Faces stopped to watch the leaves dance and tried to join them, but she could not hear the music, so she could not follow the steps. That was okay, the birds were singing. However, when she tried to whistle, she could not keep up with the beat and gave it up as well. Oh well, there was always the crown. She would look at it for a while. Then, when she turned to look at the peak, she saw a young man coming her way. He was carrying a package. *Could he be one of those who are following their destiny?* she wondered as she waited. *Then I wouldn't have to travel alone.*

"I am glad you waited," he said as he handed her the package. "I thought I would have to go all the way up to the summit to give this to you."

Many Faces was taken back by the surprise. "You mean this is for me? But, why? What is it? Who is it from? Who are you?" she asked.

"I don't have any answers," he replied. "I am only a messenger."

Many Faces sat down, ripped the box open and found a gold chalice. Like the gold box that carried Eyes with the letters inscribing faith, the chalice had letters r, t, u, h and t, which spelled the word truth. But Many Faces did not know that. When she looked up to question the messenger, he was gone.

In that same moment, a cloud came forth, lowered itself, and an angel stepped down from it. All Many Faces could do was stare, gasp, and bow. A pure sound of music then filled the air, the angel's white robe glowed, and the chalice filled with clear water. "Be not afraid, Many Faces, I am the Angel of Truth. Raise your eyes, look upon me, and then take a sip from the chalice, for no harm shall come to you."

Many Faces did as told, and as she sipped, the angel spoke. "I have come to speak on behalf of Justice, for it has been kidnapped and is now bound behind the wall of truth. When it ruled, mankind did not have faith in it, so they cast it aside and made a complex set of laws for themselves. Now they change these laws at will to use as a means to serve each end, and the end is not for rescuing our friend

Justice. Sad to say, they fail to see that those same laws keep them in bondage as well.

"But be not dismayed," the angel continued, "for all that man projects from within does not come back empty. All that is purposed for destruction will destroy him. All that is purposed for harm will harm him, and those sought after in revenge will be the avenged. Many Faces, the sole purpose of Justice is to keep the nature of man in balance as it is a law unto itself. Take the chalice with you, for each sip you take will bring to mind all you have learned on your journey."

Then a cloud came forth, covered the angel, and left Many Faces in the full splendor of her glory.

Happiness could not wait to talk to her again. She was starting to wonder who needed to see whom. Still, it was a golden moment in time. She flew right over, sat on the lip of the chalice, crossed her legs, and smiled. "Congratulations once again. You have just received one of the most valuable gifts thus far."

"Thank you, Happiness. I wish I could share in your gladness, but I am still numb."

"I know. I saw it too. It was glory at its best, wasn't it? But if it will help any, you are quite near the meadow. In fact, if there are no more stops, you should reach it by nightfall."

"That reminds me, how come you did not tell me about Mount Splendor?"

"Ahhh, that. It was because of what your friend Peace said. 'Whoever you meet along the way let it be for the sake of giving. They are your companions, and each must dream his own dream and follow his own destiny.' And you do have a destiny, my friend. Anyway, I think that you are going to love it there. Just wait until you see the flowers, fruits, and berries that grow there. They are profuse. And there is a huge lake there as well. Oops, that reminds me, I need to leave now if I am going to make it before nightfall. I'm a lot slower than you are, you know." She giggled as she left the cup and flew away.

As Many Faces watched Happiness fly away, she came to realize just how much she had grown to love her. Her sweet playful ways, the surprise visits, the way she teased, the special way she fluttered her wings, and her precious, little smiles were only a few of the things Many Faces admired so much. Then she realized just how far she had come since they first met. Her triumph over fear, loneliness and pain, her encounter with time and freedom, the gift of peace, the little side excursion into the cave (which had probably been planned), the wonders of beauty, the glory of justice, and of course, the gift of Eyes of Faith. Then it dawned on her. She had not seen Eyes of Faith since they were at the summit. Eyes of Faith, on the other hand, did not lose sight of her. They always knew where she was, and where she was going.

"Eyes," she called out. "Where are you?"

"We're right here," they replied as they glided over and winked.

"Ahhh, for a minute there, I thought I'd lost you."

"Only if you want to," they kidded.

"Next stop is the meadow, right?"

"Right. But not 'til tomorrow."

"Oh, you're right. Come to think of it, I guess I am pretty tired."

Many Faces then hugged her chalice, snuggled under the stars, and went to sleep.

# The Meadow

The sun was still asleep and the birds were just waking. It was an ideal time to leave. They would make it to the meadow in time to watch the sunrise over the lake without distraction, but they had to hurry. Eyes dashed over to Many Faces to wake her up. "Many Faces," they sparkled, "wake up."

The flash woke her and Many Faces shot straight up. "What's wrong, Eyes?"

"Nothing. I just thought you might like to be at the meadow when the sun rose."

"Are we that close?"

"Yes, it's just a hop, skip, and a jump away, and if we leave now, we should get there just in time to see it."

Many Faces stretched and yawned. "Great, I could use a sunrise bath," she giggled.

Eyes of Faith was right. It was only a hop, skip, and a jump away. The sun was just starting to rise, and that is when she saw it. Many Faces gasped. What else could she do? After being in brush and rock for so long, this had to be heaven. Sure, Happiness said that there would be flowers, fruits, and berries, but not only did the lush carpet extend from one side of the lake to the other, the fruit and berry trees were all in bloom as well. And yes, she said there was a lake, but did not say a word about its majesty. Then she saw

45

Happiness bathing in the sun, and ran straight to her. "Happiness, why didn't you tell me you lived in paradise? I imagined it to be more like a valley with more berries and fruit. And the lake. Why didn't you tell me it was so majestic?"

"Hey, good morning to you too. I see you finally made it. What happened to you last night?"

"Ah, nothing really. I got carried away with my thoughts, so Eyes suggested that we spend the night. That's all."

"That was a good idea as I barely made it back myself. You should try the water, it feels great."

"Thanks, I think I'll do just that. I really need a bath."

Many Faces squatted at the edge of the lake, stretched her hand out to the water, and quickly yanked it back. Happiness saw it. "The water is not cold. I just bathed in it and it was warm," she said.

"No, that's not it. It seems that when I touched the water, something tugged at me. Is there something in there?"

"Not that I know of," Happiness answered. "What kind of a tug was it?"

"I don't know. It was as if someone down there was asking me to dive in and save them."

Eyes of Faith knew what it was, but she could not say a word about it. Her task was to get Many Faces to learn to trust her voice and follow. "Come on, Many Faces, there's nothing to be afraid of. I will be with you. Do you not remember what Mr. Moon once said to you: 'There is something special that you alone must see?' So follow me and I will show it to you," Eyes said as they turned and dove straight in.

"Well, I suppose that there's no harm in a swim," Many Faces replied as she held her breath and plunged in after Eyes.

At first, it was fun. Then as Eyes went deeper, the cooler and darker the water became. Many Faces was now worried. How much longer could she hold her breath, or see where Eyes of Faith was going? But that did not bother Eyes of Faith. They knew exactly what to do, and when and how to do it. They burst into the light, grabbed Many Faces by the hand, and whisked her to the door of a buried tunnel. "You have to go in alone," Eyes said. "I will wait for you out here."

Many Faces grabbed the door, entered, and let out a deep breath. It surprised her. Not only could she breathe, but she could see clearly now. Then she saw him. Tall, back turned, and wearing a long white-hooded robe. His voice was like the sound of a babbling brook. "Please don't be afraid to come close to me, Many Faces, for what I have to give to you is that which you have been searching for throughout your journey."

The voice was likened to that of Time, and Many Faces went forward in peace. Then he turned and she saw his face. It too was marked with a thousand gentle lines. Many Faces froze. *Please, don't let it be Old Man Pain again*, she thought. But it wasn't.

The mysterious man reached for Many Faces, drew her close, and hugged her tight. Then, with a blink of an eye, he transformed his face to match that of hers, and filled her with a deep and peaceful love. It was that quick and simple. Many Faces then discovered the love she had yearned for was within her all along. It had always existed deep within her. She breathed a deep sigh, and smiled.

"Welcome home, Many Faces," he said. "You have just received the miraculous gift of love. Cherish it always, for though you have the gift of peace, the chalice of truth, and the Eyes of Faith, the greatest of these three is the gift of love.

"Love is the light that shines in darkness. It sees through the eyes of understanding, and is merciful to forgive all wrongdoings of self as well as those of all others and remembers them not.

"Love is patient and kind. It is not evil, but sees only the good in all of life.

"Love does not brag about what it is or what it does; it is pure. Its motives are to give of itself, to express its goodness through humanity, and to see its own reflection in all of life. Otherwise it would be just a meaningless and forgotten word.

"Love is not selfish. Therefore, when you give to others, do it for the sake of love or it will profit you nothing, for the purpose of love is but to fulfill itself in others and in life. If it were not so, life would be empty and your existence would be meaningless.

"Love will never fail you as it is the very essence that permeates the air that you breathe. It is the power by which all of life is sustained. It is in all that is or will be—for Love is."

Old Man Pain's words were confirmed. It was just as he said. It felt like a powerful flood just forced its way through the closed gates of an empty reservoir, filled it, and freed her. Many Faces knew then that all the while she sought after love, it was with her. "Please, come back with me," she urged him.

"I am not able to do that, Little One," he replied as he touched her face softly. "This is my home. I have been here since the beginning and will stay here until the end. Here, take this locket with you. It is a gift in remembrance of your journey. It contains a picture of you, and now that you have the precious Eyes of Love, each time you look inside of it, you will see that *you are the gold, and love is within your heart*. Promise me you will always remember that." He clasped the locket around her neck.

The embrace was long and tender. It had to be. It was their last. "I promise," Many Faces, said as they parted. "I will always keep it close to my heart."

The light in Eyes of Faith was brilliant and ascent was quick and safe. One look from Eyes told Many Faces that they knew what had just happened. They glistened, winked, and left her to be with Happiness, who had been waiting to applaud her. She flew right over, motioned her wings, and clapped. "Congratulations! Now you really have the whole world in your hands. Come on, let's play tag to celebrate."

"Not right now, Happiness. I have just received the greatest gift in the universe and I want to lay here and bask in it for awhile."

"As you wish. But don't forget, I won't be here all day," she teased.

"That's okay. Remember you were the one who said that eventually I would not need to see you as much. Besides, now that I have finally found what I have been searching for, I will be the one to stay. So, for a change, I'll be the one to congratulate you each time you come back home."

However, what Many Faces did not know was that she would never see Happiness again.

# Part II

# The Land of Forgotten

Happiness and Mr. Dove flew back up to Mount Splendor. They knew Eyes of Faith would be at the crest, and it was urgent that they find them.

"Eyes, we need to talk to you. It is urgent," Happiness said.

Eyes of Faith turned and blinked. "What's wrong?"

"It's Many Faces. She has gone off the deep end."

Eyes panicked. "Do you mean to say she drowned?"

"No, I mean that after she received the Eyes of Love, all she did was swim, eat, sleep, sunbathe, pick flowers, and moon over the stars. She was happy."

"Yes, and peaceful too," Mr. Dove nodded.

"Then one day, she quit! Just like that!" Happiness flipped her wings back and forth in a quick snap. "Now all she does is sit and stare out at water all day. She will not eat nor will she drink from the gold chalice! We have both tried to talk to her, but all she does is ignore us. It is as if we don't even exist."

"So what do you want me to do," Eyes of Faith asked.

"Well, we thought if the three of us went down to talk to her, maybe she would listen."

"Ahhh, come on guys, you know better than to mess with destiny. Why do you think I left? Remember, you guys are free to come and go as you please, but I'm not. I have to wait for her to call on me before I can help."

"That's true," Happiness nodded. "It's just sad to see her like this, that's all."

"Yeah, I know. Stay here with me. She'll call, you'll see," Eyes replied.

"Thanks all the same, but we have to go. Mr. Dove has an appointment and I want to go back down and see what Many Faces is doing. I am real worried about her."

"Me too," Eyes of Faith nodded.

Many Faces held the locket and stared at the sad eyes in the picture. It was her all right; nevertheless, she was sure that she had been deceived. The pain was back and there was no one to turn to. "Oh sure, you're the gold and love is within your heart. Humph! What a farce," she growled. "Oooh, and then there's the Great Elusive. *'I have to share myself with all who follow their destiny,'*" she mimicked. "She is just as much of an illusion as all else is. And what about this 'being friends with yourself' stuff that good ol' Mr. Loneliness told me I had to do? What good has that done? Humph! Well, I am tired of being friends with myself! And this love is within your heart stuff! Ha! That's another good one! Where does that have me? Nowhere, that's where."

She snarled. "What a mistake it was to leave the cave. The cave people were right. Just think, had I listened to them, I would not be in this predicament. But maybe if I go back the same way I came, I can find them again."

Many Faces picked up the chalice, grabbed the locket, and hurled them both into the water. She watched them sink and then walked away.

It was too late. Happiness did not get back in time to stop her. "Many Faces, please come back," she shouted. "You need to have the chalice and locket with you! Why did you have to go and do that? You will be lost without them for sure."

Eyes of Faith heard the calls of Happiness and flew down to be with her. "And what about us," they cried. "I was the one who guided her out of The Land of Many Trees, taught her how to close her eyes to the great temptation of collecting for the sake of greed, and guided her out of the cave, up the mountain, and through the water. I don't know what she will do now."

"But she has to come back, doesn't she, Eyes?"

"Yes, Happiness, she will be back, but she will not be the same," they sadly replied.

The back track failed and now she was stuck. There were no trees, no Mount Splendor, and no cave. Many Faces came out at the wrong end of the meadow and was now at a fork. The path in front was straight. The one on the left went around a sharp bend, and the one on the right curved up a hill and then disappeared over the top. She blinked and stared.

"Hmmm, it looks like I'm on my own now. I wonder what I should do. I know, I'll just close my eyes and pick." Many Faces shut her eyes, stretched her arm, and pointed. "Eenie, Meenie, Miney, Mo. Tell me which way I should go."

"You obviously want the straight one," a voice answered gruffly.

Many Faces turned and saw no one. "Who is there?"

"It's me and I'm up here," the vulture replied.

"Hey, you're back!"

"Yeah, but only because I thought you would never make it to the fork."

"What do mean by that?"

"Oh, never mind. Just take the straight path. I will explain it to you later," it said as it flew away.

"There he goes again and I don't even know who he is. No matter—I will do what he said." Many Faces shrugged, sighed, and then smiled. Now she was happy that the back track failed. She was on a new path, confident and glad to be free. No mountains or rocks to climb over, and no brush or trees in the way. In fact, this way did not take long at all. It was straight and easy.

Then it appeared. A small town set in the horizon. "I knew it," she squealed. "I knew I could do it. Just think, no more long and lonely nights, and I won't need to imagine shadows, doves, trees, flowers, or flying eyes to talk to. What a fool I've been. No wonder the cave people laughed at me. And with good reason too. If I had listened to them, I would be secure and happy by now. It doesn't matter. I won't make that mistake again. No sir, this time, I'm going to listen."

Red blazed on the horizon, then turned violet, then to grey and that meant that Many Faces had to hurry if she was to be there by nightfall. She began to run as fast as she could, but it was too late. The dark caught her in the middle of a thickset of trees. She groped through the thicket, pushed through the rugged brush, scratched her arms, tore her dress and then, as if it knew that Many Faces needed help, the city burst forth in radiance and lit the final pass for her. There it was, clear as day, the stone arched gateway to happiness— or so she thought.

Desperate for a warm place to sleep, Many Faces gathered up what little strength she had left, stormed the path, neared the gate, and collapsed on the cold, hard ground. She lay helpless to move for what may have been minutes or hours before she could crawl the few feet that were left. Both her legs and arms hurt from the scratches and her breathing was heavy.

That isn't what bothered her, however. What bothered her was the size of the gates. There were two, and each one was about seven and half feet wide, made of wrought iron and opened outward. *Where would she get the strength to pull?*

Many Faces took in a deep breath, gripped a bar to pull herself up, and peered through. Her intentions were simple, sneak in quietly and find a place to sleep. *Good—the streets are empty and all is quiet*, she thought.

As Many Faces began to pull, a line of knights on white horses suddenly came trotting through the inner court. Many Faces quickly jumped back and crouched down. As a crowd began to gather, the line of knights split—one half circling to the left, the other to the right, and then they enclosed the crowd.

This was a nightly routine for them. The men dressed in their best, the women put on their finest gowns, garnished themselves with jewels, and met in the square to stroll and see who outdid who. They never spoke, just nodded to the left and then to the right as they passed each other.

The realism of the state she was in hit Many Faces hard and all of her hopes and dreams vanished. *Now what am I going to do? All I have is this one filthy torn dress! I am dirty, my feet are callused from going barefoot for so long, and I am tired and homeless.* She began to sob as she slowly walked back out into the lone night.

King Ekaf was born short, and he was always mad at the Gods for it. He had thinning brown hair, close-set beady eyes, and an extra large nose, which made him even angrier. Apart from being arrogant, cunning, and rude, he was also schooled in the art of betrayal. An expert at controlling others, and he appeased no one but himself.

He was a slave to his God Money, to his Master Time, and he loved to rule his Kingdom with an iron fist. He kept prisons full with those who tried to flee his ruthless grip. He had to—there was no choice. These prisoners were what Ekaf used for the daily sacrifice to the Gods. Old or young, men, women or children, it didn't matter. "You fly, you die," was his motto.

From the moment Many Faces came near the gate, Ekaf had seen her, and was only watching to see what she would do next. When Many Faces turned to walk away, he jumped up, grabbed his horse, and went after her. "Move aside," he yelled, pushing those who did not move at his first request. He knew it would be easy to find her as there was no place to hide. He had cut down all of the trees and brush to make it easy for the Legion to look for the outcasts.

He scanned the grounds. Just as he thought, there she was lying asleep on the ground only a few feet ahead of him. Ekaf left his horse and slowly tiptoed the rest of the way, then he crouched down and studied her. She was still breathing. He gently poked her on the shoulder a few times to see if she would move, but Many Faces did not budge. She was out cold.

"Astonishing, she almost looks human," he almost whispered. "Now why would this strange, frail creature come to our city, stare as if we were the strange ones, and then go to sleep on the dirt? She can't be one of my slaves, unless she escaped from the prison of the poor. No, that can't be it," he shook his head. "They know better than to try and escape. Aside from that, I would have known about it. But she sure does look like one of them. On the other hand, she could be wearing a mask."

Now, Ekaf was suspicious. He wanted to pull the skin on her face to check and see if she wore one, but decided he would do it later. He knew what his plan was, and for the time being, he would keep her under close observation. "At least I am sure she is not a runaway slave. Thus, finder's keepers! Cleaned up, she will make me a good prize," he chortled. Ekaf then went back to the palace. Picking out a large imitation red rose, he went back, tossed it near her head and left. "This will not take long," he mumbled.

The dew soaked through her thin, torn dress and a cold chill ran through her. Many Faces opened her eyes and stared at the parade of thoughts that streamed out from her mind. Had what she had seen the night before been real, or was it imagined? Many Faces wasn't sure. The only thing she was sure of was that she was back out in the cold.

She turned, saw the gate, bolted straight up, and rushed from stump to stump trying to hide. "Wait a minute," she told herself. "Calm down, there is no need to panic. It was too dark for anyone to see me." She relaxed, walked back, saw the fake rose and picked it up. *Hmmm—it's a fake flower. This must be a good omen,* she thought, *I think I'll go check it out again.*

Many Faces kept her eye on the gate, and to check to be sure that she was not seen or followed, she slouched like a nervous hound, tiptoed forward, checked from left to right, and then behind until she reached the gate. Then she took one last check, slithered against the wall, and peered in.

She blinked as she stared at the bare streets in disbelief. "There was a gala in here last night, of that I am sure," she whispered, still staring. "Now there is not a soul. Good, this might be part of the good omen."

Many Faces pulled the gate, tiptoed through, and stood still. All was quiet. "This is odd," she barely whispered. "They could not have all just vanished! Maybe it was a dream. No, this square was filled with people last night—I saw them!"

Then it hit her. She was standing on top of a gold paved street. How could she have missed it? When the sun hit it, it was blinding. "My God, just look at all of this gold!"

Now she was gripped. The door to her heart slammed shut and a deep seed of lust took over. She had to make a plan. She was sure that if she went back each night to watch, memorize and practice all she saw them do, she could slip in and no one would notice. That seemed easy enough. In the meantime, she would rest until dark.

The king knew exactly what she was going to do. Too many had already tried it. He would rest until dark as well. Each night he dropped a rose next to her head and kept an eye on her all day. Just as he thought, it did not take long at all. The moves were perfect and the avarice was in place. Now he could bring the package—she was ready.

Many Faces woke to a new fake rose each day. Today she turned as usual to reach for it, saw the package that someone had left for her in the night, and shot straight up. Not once did it occur to her that someone knew what she was up to, nor that someone had been spying, scheming, and planning to move in on her like a trapped, hungry dog.

Nonetheless, Many Faces grabbed the package and ripped it open. It was a gown—an exact copy of one she had seen the women wear. Then it dawned on her, she had been exposed. But, by whom, for what purpose, when, and why had she not noticed? On the one hand, she was grateful; on the other, she was annoyed.

Many Faces threw the gown down and stood up. "Come out where I can see you," she called. No one answered. "Darn," she grumbled. That means I have to hide behind the stupid stump all day, wait for nightfall, and pretend to sleep so I can find out who it is." She picked up her gown, walked over to the stump, and sat down.

Closing her eyes, she let her mind drift free. It went back to the night she first peered through the gates, only it was she who was wearing the jewelled gown and standing among the crowd, nodding to the left, then to the right with all eyes fixed upon her. The line of white horses came trotting through the inner court. As they split, one of the knights saw her, and as he neared, he reached down, grabbed her by the waist, and whisked her up on his white horse. The crowd cheered and clapped. Many Faces nestled up to the knight in shining armor, and smiled.

The sound of footsteps snapped Many Faces out of her dream. She quickly crawled back to her bed, closed her eyes, and laid still. It was dark. King Ekaf tiptoed over, crouched as usual, and put the small sack next to her head. Many Faces could feel the scrutiny. It was now or never. She turned her head, squinted, and broke the silence. "Hello there," she whispered softy. Instinctively for both, Ekaf grabbed the sack and jumped up, and Many Faces bolted to her feet. "Please don't leave," she pleaded as she reached for him.

"Don't touch me," he shouted. "I am a king!"

Stunned, Many Faces bowed and froze.

"Here, clean yourself up," he growled as he threw both a mask and the small sack of grooming supplies at her feet. "You are a mess and you need to look decent before you speak to me."

Many Faces had no choice but to obey. She had not met a king before, but the sharp tone told her she had better do as he asked. She picked up the sack and took out a hairbrush, a wet cloth, and a mask. She quickly washed, put on the gown and brushed her hair. "What should I do with this?" she asked, holding up the mask.

"Put it on."

"I don't understand. Why do I need to wear a mask?"

Ekaf shifted his weight and folded his arms. "Come, sit here at my feet while I explain how you will be expected to behave as one who is fortunate enough to be chosen as the noble maiden of one of the mightiest, and most handsome I might add, kings in this land. One of the most basic requirements is to never be seen in public without a mask. Therefore, you must comply at once."

Many Faces was more than stunned now. Who would ever think that she, Many Faces, could go from a pauper to a princess overnight? She quickly grabbed the mask and did as the king commanded.

"Good," he said. "Now, aside from that basic rule, we will start by giving you a new name. How does Maiden Eslaf sound? It has a nice ring to it, don't you think? Good, so be it! Now, Maiden Eslaf, in my kingdom, which will soon be yours, the second most important rule is—"

"But my name is Many Faces," she protested.

King Ekaf was mad. He pounded his chest and yelled. "I am the great King Ekaf who rules the Land of Forgotten! You did not

58

choose me, I chose you! And if I say your name is Maiden Eslaf, that is what it is. Furthermore, you will now address me as my Lord! Got it?"

Many Faces hunched and trembled. "Yes, my Lord."

Ekaf looked down at her and squinted. "By the way, what kingdom did you come from?" He knew that she would lie. Many Faces had to hide her fear of rejection.

"Why do you ask me that, my Lord?"

"How dare you answer me with a question!" he snapped.

"Forgive me, my Lord, what I meant to say was that in the kingdom of The Land of Many Trees, we did not have rules or wear masks, but I have heard about rules."

"Ha! Every one wears a mask."

"Yes, my Lord."

King Ekaf squinted as he planned his next move. He loved to be intimidating—not that he needed to be. Many Faces was too naive to understand what he was doing or saying to her, and Ekaf already knew that she was in the palm of his hand. However, he had no choice since he needed to use the weakness of others to hide his own.

He helped Many Faces to her feet and patted her on the back. "Come and sit with me," he said, as he led her back to where she slept. "You see my little maiden, in my kingdom, if you want to belong, you must do exactly as I say. The first thing is that you must never take your mask off in public. If you do, you will be exiled from my Kingdom."

The very thought of being aimless and confused scared her. Many Faces promised herself that it would not ever happen again. "Yes, my Lord," she nodded.

Ekaf saw the change, but ignored it. "As I was saying, in my Kingdom, our status is based on the mask, and since each mask projects how we want to be perceived by others, we must be careful which one we choose to wear."

"What do you mean by that, my Lord?"

"Why, the mask, of course," he grumped. "Each one is an integral part of our identity, so each mask we choose to wear is the one we perceive ourselves to be at the time we wear it. The real trick is to make others see us the way we want them to see us. We call it a 'perceived identity' since it is one and the same with each one of the masks that we wear."

"What is a perceived identity, my Lord?"

Ekaf turned red, slammed his fist, and raised his voice. "Look. It is simple! Others see us the way we want them to see us, and we choose the mask that projects the image we want to project. That's all!"

His lack of patience did not bother Many Faces one bit. What bothered her was her failure to grasp what he said. "Do you mean that each mask is an identity?"

"Of course! Don't you know that you can be whatever you want to be with each mask?"

"You can?"

"Yes, each one is a piece of your identity which is merely a simple perception of the mind."

"A perception of the mind?" She blinked.

"Sure. You see, a single perception is a sum of distinct perceptions. That is to say, each perception is separate, but as they flow, they create an effect as one. It is sort of like a river, except the river is not the illusion. The flow of the perception is. Simply put, if you want others to see you in the way you want them to, then you have to control their perceptions, ergo the mask. What is significant is that once you wear it, you become it. For example, now that you wear your Maiden Eslaf mask, you will act like one, my people will perceive you as one, and then they will treat you as such. You see how simple it is," he grinned.

Many Faces got lost in all of the gobbledygook the king spewed. She did not know how in the world she was to understand this new mumbo jumbo. On the one hand, she wanted to hurry up and get it over with so they could get going, and on the other, she did not want to make herself look like she was not interested in what he had to say. Moreover, she had to factor in the fear. "I'm sorry, my Lord, but I didn't understand a word you said. I mean—"

"What do you mean you didn't understand a word of it? It is elementary! Look, now that you wear a new mask, you have a new identity. Period!" he growled.

"You mean this mask makes me a real maiden?"

"Well, sort of. That is to say, when you wear it, you project to others that you are a maiden. Then, because they treat you like one, you come to believe it as well, and voila! You have a new identity!"

"Ohh, now I get it! That is simple, my Lord."

"Yes, it is. That is what I have been trying to tell you. My kingdom does not allow the imperfect to be exposed, thus it is masked."

"But then isn't that deceiving? I mean, if it is only a mask, then doesn't that fake the identity of those who wear it, which in turn fools the perceptions?"

"Absolutely not," he barked. "On the contrary, truth lies in what you see. The mask creates the effect of perfection, and that is the true reality. Can't you see the beauty in it? If one cannot see the imperfect, then it does not exist."

It was her only chance. No way was she about to blow being a king's maiden. So what if she did not understand a word he said. Many Faces fixed her mask and nodded. "Yes, my Lord, that is smart."

"I thought you might see it my way, Maiden Eslaf. By the way, you need to know that the perceived identity is the only criterion we use for social placement in my kingdom. Therefore, if you want to keep your status and your identity, it is imperative that you do exactly as I say. Got it?"

"Yes, my Lord, I will do exactly as you say. I promise you, I will not disappoint you."

That is what Ekaf was waiting to hear. He lifted her gown, reached for her thigh, and squeezed it. Many Faces squirmed, but said nothing. "That we shall see, my maiden; you've yet to prove yourself to me. Come, it's time for you to lay with me in my palace." He stood and pulled her to her feet. The flat stare of detachment that was part of the mask was now set. Many Faces stood, raised her chin, and became one with Maiden Eslaf.

# The Lost Kingdom

I t was better than her dream. As was the custom, the knights were in line at the gates when they opened. As King Ekaf and Many Faces rode through, the knights raised their lances to salute them. The crowd parted, cheered, and secretly wondered just how long the king's new toy would last. Ekaf circled the square, dismounted, pulled Many Faces down from the waist, grabbed her by the arm, and headed for the palace.

Many Faces knew the routine. Eyes fixed dead ahead, lids down, chin up, nod to the left and then to the right. *This is not a dream anymore,* she thought. *Just think—me, Many Faces, a real noble maiden. Boy, those long hours of practice sure paid off!*

Ekaf stopped in front of the court to his palace. "You can't walk across this yet," he said as he turned, lifted her off her feet, and set her down before a large crystal capsule filled with gold coins. "You need to pay homage to your new God Money first. Kneel and bow, then you may walk across it yourself."

Many Faces knelt, bowed, and then stood and circled it. It looked to be about eight feet high, four feet around, and shaped like a time bottle. "This is my new God? But it is only a time bottle," she frowned.

Ekaf's face blazed red. He turned, grabbed her shoulders, and shook her as if she were a rag doll. The grip was tight. "Don't you ever say that again! Time is Money and they are both my Gods! And if you are to stay, you will love, honor, and obey us with all of your heart, mind, and soul. Do you understand," he screamed shaking her.

Many Faces' head bounced back and forth like an ill fit spring. The shock and pain was quick. "Yes! I mean yes, my Lord, I do! I mean yes, my Lord, I will. I promise. Only I beg of you, please stop," she cried.

His rage passed, Ekaf let go and Many Faces fell on her knees and trembled. "Good. Herein, you will kneel and bow each time that you pass this altar. You got it?"

"Yes, my Lord," she sniffled.

Ekaf squinted and eyed her. He did not feel one bit of remorse. *She will do as I say and that is that,* he thought. "That's what I like to hear. The God of our Kingdom is the almighty God Money, the Lord who reigns, is Lord Time, and they and I are one. Got it?"

"Yes, my Lord."

"Look for yourself," he said as he waved his arms over the palace. "All of this is from him, Eslaf. All you have to do is please us, and the more you do that, the more power and wealth he will bestow on us. That is the Golden Rule, he who has the gold—rules. Now then, when we go to the offering in the morning, you will see a large gold tower, and at the foot, you will see a long table with a tabernacle on it. That is where we meet to make the sacrifices to God each day."

"Yes, my Lord," she nodded.

"Good. Now get up. It is almost dawn, and you still have a duty to perform."

It was the law. Get up at dawn, pray, and then rush off to make the sacrifice for the day. Ekaf was the only one who knew what God demanded from them. If they wanted peace, they sacrificed the little people, an increase in wealth, the aged, and to pledge allegiance, they gave up their friends. He consulted with Lord Time and gave the edict to the Council. They saw it through, the knights brought them to the altar, and the people followed.

It was that simple, but how was Many Faces supposed to know all of that? Ekaf had not told her yet. When she woke and found him gone, she panicked. Dressing quickly, she grabbed her mask, rushed out of the palace, and found him at the statue. He was kneeling. "My Lord, I thought that you'd—"

Ekaf clenched his teeth tight, jumped up, and slapped her hard. Then he grabbed her nape and pushed her to her knees. Her mask went flying and Ekaf picked it up and threw it at her. "When will you learn? Mask on, kneel, bow, and don't ever interrupt me here again," he screamed.

The blow stung hard. Many Faces grabbed the mask and put it on as fast as she could. In a way she was grateful, it hid her pain. "Please forgive me, my Lord. I will never do it again—I swear," she replied coldly.

"Let us hope not. Now come on, let's get going."

They were a few minutes late. A gold time capsule towered nine feet or more high above the square. Ekaf pushed his way through the crowd and Many Faces followed like a servant. The incident was still fresh in his mind and he was still cranky. He gripped her arm and yanked her close. Many Faces tripped. "Look, you better walk straight next to me, hold your head high, and act like the rest of us," he scowled.

As the sound of drums beat loud in the distance, they moved to the front and stood at the foot of the table. It was about five feet high and four feet wide, and the tabernacle in the center looked about three feet high, and two feet wide. Oval-shaped, it was coated with dark blue sapphires. A group of seven men wearing—long, black robes and small, round black caps—stood side by side behind it. The one in the middle had a high, round black cap and held a large, silver-bound book to his chest. "These men are from the Council and the one with the book is the High Bishop," Ekaf whispered. "Pay close attention, the peace offering will be here in a minute."

"Yes, my Lord," she nodded.

The knights marched in line, and the beat of the drums grew louder. The crowd roared and cheered as they passed through. Many Faces stayed silent. King Ekaf poked her in the rib with his elbow. "Cheer," he mumbled.

Then Many Faces saw the group of shackled children being hauled behind them. The drums stopped and the crowd went silent. As the High Bishop stepped forward, the knights clicked their heels, raised their lances, and saluted. Many Faces turned to look at the crowd, and then looked back at Ekaf. They all had the same cold, hard look. She touched her mask, frowned, and wondered if she looked the same.

"Is this all of them?" the High Bishop asked.

"Yes, your Honor," the general bellowed as he handed him a rolled parchment.

"Are all the names of the donors listed?"

"Yes, your Honor."

"Good. Then bring them up."

"Who are those children and what are they going to do with them, my Lord," Many Faces finally asked.

"That, Maiden Eslaf, is the peace offering. They are going to be sacrificed to God for the sake of peace."

"But why? Have they been bad?"

Ekaf thought for a minute. He had to keep it simple, which meant extra work and that in and of itself goaded him. "It's His law, that's why!" he snapped. "Don't you remember me saying that the more we please Him, the more power and wealth he bestows?"

"Yes, my Lord."

"Well, one of the ways we please Him is to offer up the 'little people,' and is only one of the sacrifices that we have to make."

"You mean there are more?"

"Yes, we have a list to go by. Everyone has to give up something to prove our love to God. Some give up more than others, but nonetheless, we all have to do it. It all depends on what God asks for. It goes like this. The knights round up the donations, turn them over to the Council whose job it is to put them into homogeneous groups, log the names of the donors in the book, and then ship them off to prison. There they are stored until such time my Lord Time shows me what sacrifice needs to made next. Then I give the edict. Understand?"

"Yes, of course," she nodded.

Ekaf twitched and pointed at the children with his chin. "They were brought here from the Prison of Small. Once the High Bishop goes over the list, the Council will log the names, and then the ceremony will start. This peace offering is for us, but the one God delights in is the offering of devotion, which is the one that we use for the pledge of allegiance.

"This is how it works," he explained. "Befriend the trusting, get what you can out of them, and then betray them. It's that simple. The reward is threefold. First, it proves our love to God. Second, it keeps our Kingdom strong in character, and third, the donor gets a palace filled with rich treasures, all of the leftovers from the one that was betrayed, and a sharp barrister to protect them from those who are trying to do the same to them." He laughed.

Many Faces' brows furrowed as she questioned. "That is a good motive to use for making friends. But if to have a friend means to be a friend, then how do you betray yourself?"

"Good God! Where did you get ever get such a stupid idea like that? Don't you know that friendship implies trust? You cannot trust anyone, not even yourself. We can only trust God, Money, and our Lord Time. Otherwise, we die!"

"Well, that's not so bad. At least it frees you."

Ekaf shook his head and glared. The law of the land was clear on this. Men thought, women asked. Men talked, women listened. Men ruled, women obeyed—and that was that. "Now hear this for I shall not repeat it to you again. I talk—you listen, and I command—you obey. That's how it works here. Otherwise, the next time will make what you made me do this morning feel like a mother's caress. Got it?"

Many Faces cringed at the thought of it. There was no way that would happen again, at least not if she could help it. "Yes, my Lord," she humbly bowed.

"Now, where was I," he grumped. "As I said, Lord Time collects donations; the Council puts them in homogeneous groups and then ships them off to prison. Can you remember that?"

"Yes, my Lord."

Ekaf thought for a minute. Should he, or shouldn't he? Would she or wouldn't she? He needed her for this. He hoped that she would grasp what he was about to say and not end up frustrated by it. He would try to be as patient as he could and hope for the best. Ekaf bent close and whispered, "Come here, I want to tell you something. It is somewhat tricky, but this is where you can help me out. Now, God requires us to make many sacrifices to Him, right?"

"Right," she replied.

"Thus, each offering made to Him has to be for a different one, right?"

"Right," she nodded.

"And each donor gets a reward each time their offering is used as a sacrifice, right?"

"Right," she nodded.

*So far so good,* he thought. "Now listen. There is a way in which one can be exalted forever, and this—is what I am after. Here is how it works. Since the donor is rewarded each time his offering is used as a sacrifice, and since they are kept track of, then obviously, it is better to donate one of many instead of many of one. That way, one gets all of the rewards, plus your name is written in the silver book. Lord Time turns you into an idol, places you in the Chamber of Immortals, and pays homage to you forever. This by far, is the highest honor that any one in my kingdom can have, and though it has been achieved by a small handful, it is prized by all."

Ekaf puffed out his chest, inhaled deeply," and continued. "I can just see it now. The famous King Ekaf the Great, the most revered in the history of the Land of Forgotten. Did you get all of that?" he asked in a low whisper.

"I think so, but I'm not sure. Are you saying that the offerings used for the sacrifice are the actual people?"

"God, I should have known better. Of course, they are, stupid! The offering used to bring us peace is the little people. To show our devotion, it is the betrayed ones, and to worship, we give Him the weak, the outcasts, and the aged. These last three are worthy of note, especially the aged. Inasmuch as the Council does not consider them in the final count, they strip them of their wealth, give it to the knights, and then ship them off to Deshart. That way, the knights are paid, and we rid the Kingdom of a good portion of the weak in one fell swoop.

"Keep in mind," he went on, "that the Lord only loves the strong and the perfect, which is why the tint skins are ousted. Their skins are sordid to look at. Some are a reddish brown, some are dark brown, and some are murky yellow. What is most notable about this last group is that their eyes slant, and not even a mask can hide that! A few of them do manage to sneak by us, but they are usually trapped by the 'body-tenders'.

"Be careful of this unit, Maiden Eslaf, they work out of the Palace of Perfection, which is where you will be spending most of your time when we get back. Their job is to seek and destroy, and they use a potion that plays tricks with the mind to do it with."

Ekaf burst out laughing. "I just love it. Those who take it believe that it can elevate their mind to the same realm as ours, and the weak and tint skins want to be so much like us that they are the first to fall."

Perhaps she was too busy memorizing the words to see the irony in it, or perhaps she did and chose to ignore it. In any case, Many Faces was too deep in the laughter to watch the troops march away, or to hear the final shrieks of the little people as the swift daggers plunged into their breasts at the end of the ceremony. All she heard was "Come on, let's go to the Palace of Pleasure for the celebration," as the king grabbed her by the arm and walked away.

At a fast pace, it was five minutes by foot, at a slow one, ten. Ekaf knew all of the shortcuts, so at a normal pace it took them less than five minutes to get there. With the exception of the mark on the front door, the palaces were all built the same—thick square stone, two stories high, with one wood double door. All windows faced the square, and all courtyards had an eight-foot tall crystal time capsule in the center.

When they arrived, there was still a long line at the capsule. "Move aside!" Ekaf shouted. The crowd jumped back and waved him through. He turned to see what Many Faces would do. She learned fast, nodding at the crowd as she passed, kneeled, and bowed at the capsule. Then, for an added touch, she turned, took Ekaf's hand, kissed it while still on her knees. It was a pleasant surprise to him and he turned to the crowd and smiled smugly.

The screams were loud as the door shut behind them, and the words of Old Man Pain came rushing to her mind: I am a friend to those who do not run from me for their height of joy will be equal to their depth of pain.

Ekaf turned. "Don't worry, those are not screams of real pain; they are screams of the pain of too much pleasure." He winked. "And from the little I got out of you last night, you better learn how to scream and squirm if you want to please me. And you better do it fast," he added as they walked down a long, dark and narrow hallway.

"Yes, my Lord. I will."

"In this kingdom, my little fair maiden, the women serve the men. Just as we must obey all of the commands of our Lord and our God, so too must you obey all of ours. We follow God's rules and you follow ours. God does with us as he pleases, and we do to you as we please. First God, then man—it is that simple."

"Yes, my Lord."

"Then make sure it is. After we leave here, you will be sent to the Hall of Learning where you will be taught by a group of elite men on how to dress to please us, what we like and dislike, when to speak, what and how we like to be served, how to please us in bed, and how to keep your place. Once you are proficient at this, you will be the perfect mate. For now, you will simply listen to what I say, and do it."

"Yes, my Lord," she nodded.

The king's favorite room was at the end of the hall. The music was loud, and the room was dim and crowded when they entered. One side was filled with large floor pillows, the other had a long table filled with food and drink. Half-clothed women danced in the center. Ekaf found a lone spot in the corner, walked over, sat and pulled her down. "Now, since this is your first time, I don't want you to do anything but listen, watch, and learn. Okay?" he whispered.

"Yes, my Lord," she nodded.

"Aside from my appetite for wealth and power, I also have a big one for that." He pointed to the dancers with his chin. "Now see those moves?"

"Yes, my Lord," she nodded.

"That is what you need to do to stimulate and please me. After all, that is what you are here for, isn't it?"

"Yes, my Lord," she nodded.

"No offering can please me more than the one you give me in bed."

"Would that be the love offering to you, my Lord?"

Ekaf looked at her and scowled. "Love? What kind of a word is that?"

Many Faces tensed as she adjusted her mask. "I don't know. I have only heard it mentioned once. But they say it is a feeling of the heart and that it makes you want to give freely."

"You do have a twisted mind, don't you? There is no such thing as to give freely. What you did was to confuse the term 'heart' with the word 'mind.' Therefore, for the sake of language, henceforth you will refer to the term 'heart' as the 'mind.' Furthermore, this uh, 'feeling' of the heart, as you so carelessly put it, means the same as to have a weak mind, and to have a weak mind means to be imperfect. Now, I don't know how many times I have to tell you this. In my Kingdom, imperfection is not acceptable, and those who do not conform to my standards are outcasts. And you do remember what we do with those, don't you?"

"Yes, my Lord."

"Furthermore, this 'thing' that you mistakenly called a 'feeling' is a mere perception of the mind. It does not make anyone want to give anything freely, and is in fact at the core of one of our games. It goes like this. The person to whom you give something doesn't know you know that it is a mere perception. Thus, they believe they obtain what they want from you, when in fact it is the other way around. This is the game of manipulation. Did you get all that?"

What else was she to do but nod yes. "It is quite a challenge," he continued. "As it sharpens both your perceptive and manipulative skills, you get what you want from the other person without their knowledge of it. It also weeds out the weak and makes the game more stimulating. It is usually played between two partners of the opposite sex; however, they can be one and the same. It all depends on if there is a chemical reaction or not.

"The object of the game," he continued, "is to gain control of the player through manipulation. If you win, you may donate the loser to the Palace of Imperfection for an extra mark in the silver book, or you may make him your slave. Should the winner choose the latter, the loser must give all the winner asks of him to give, and get nothing in return.

71

"Now the rules are quite simple. No displeasure can be given; each player has the right to expect a reward for any pleasurable stimulus that is given—that is, if it is received as such; and both have the right to expect complete obedience in spite of the request that is made from them.

"And last, but not least, females bound by contract are not allowed to play—and that means you."

"Yes, my Lord."

Then the beat of the music increased. The men began to shout, clap, and whistle as they watched the dancers strip down to the bare. The moment was near. Ekaf leaned back on the pillow, slipped his hand up Many Faces' leg, and squeezed it. "Now watch this," he said. Sweat streamed down the dancers' faces and bellies as their hips moved to the rhythm of the beat.

Then it stopped, the wet dancers slid to the floor, and the men all rushed them. King Ekaf pushed Many Faces down and said, "Now show me what you learned."

# Part III

# The Ascent

The years passed, and the void grew deeper. But how would Many Faces know that? She was numb. She dressed, screamed, squirmed, spoke, laughed, spied, betrayed, nodded, kneeled, and gave King Ekaf little people to sacrifice. She collected the weak, the aged, and the tint skins for him and for his God. Ekaf said jump and she said how high.

The amount of donations assured him a place in the Chamber and now he was bored with her, but he could not exchange her. She was too good at what she did and he did not feel like training a new one. Then he had an idea. He would use her sexual skills in his favor. He would lend her to his men and while they were busy with her, he could skill all the others. That way, he could get out of his sexual rut, his men would be satisfied, Many Faces would be out of his hair, and he would end up the hero.

The plan worked well for a short time. The trouble was that Many Faces began to feel lonely, depressed, and tired, which was good in the sense that at least she felt something. However, today would be different. Many Faces would not go to the Palace of Pleasure; she would go home, get some sleep, and have a dream.

Many Faces was out cold when the dream came. She was back in Paradise, and it was just as she left it. The lush carpet of flowers was in bloom, trees were filled with fruit, and the blue lake glimmered under the bright sun. Then she saw her—Elusive, the Great Golden Butterfly of Happiness—sitting on a flower.

Many Faces was elated to see her. "Happiness," she called out as she chased her. But Happiness vanished and Many Faces was thrown into the middle of a thick, black forest. It was dark and eerie. The sound of leaves rustled in the background. If only she could tell what it was, she would not feel so scared.

As the sound of the rustle grew closer, Many Faces' heart beat louder. She turned just in time to see a big black bear come up behind her. The shrill of her scream echoed through the night as she ran.

"Wait," yelled the bear. "I must talk to you." No way was she going to believe that. Bears are not friendly. That she knew. Worse yet, each time Many Faces looked back at it, it slowed her down and the bear got closer. Suddenly, a sharp pain cut through her shins and she fell facedown. The bear would now eat her for sure. All she hoped for was that it would be quick and painless.

Then it was over. Many Faces woke in a cold sweat, shot straight up, fumbled for her mask, and dropped it. It did not matter. It was dark, Ekaf was gone, and no one would see her. Many Faces lit a torch, went to the bath, saw her face in the mirror, and heard the same sharp shrill. It shook her to the core. It was she. Her eyes were cold and hard, the sockets were deep, and her mouth and nose deformed.

Many Faces threw the torch at the mirror and shattered it. But that did not change a thing. Her face was real, and so was the knot in her gut. Then it hit her. Her life was a fake and she was a fraud. It was all in the name. How could she have missed it? Ekaf spelled fake, and Eslaf spelled false. She slammed the door, rushed out of the palace, passed the Time Capsule, ran out of the gates and into the lone, cold night.

Many Faces could not shake off the look of the ugly face that she had seen in the mirror. The faster she ran, the faster it came. There was no place to hide. Many Faces was doomed, of that she was sure. Then the same sharp pain in her dream hit her shin and knocked her to the ground. The cut was deep, but the pain that cut through her soul was worse. The vile thoughts of her past made her heave, and no matter how much she heaved, the memories played on. The simple heave did not erase them. Only death could do that, and Many Faces begged for it to take her.

A cool breeze then came through and whispered her name. It was like a déjà vu for Many Faces. She buried her face in the dirt and waited for the end to come. But it wasn't a dream and it wasn't the bear. It was the man whose face was marked with a thousand gentle lines, only this time, he was brokenhearted. "Many Faces, please look up at me," he gently said.

The voice of Old Man Pain angered her. She wanted to see death, not more pain. "No," she screamed. "Leave me alone, for it is death that I seek."

Old Man Pain shook his head. "You have forgotten much, little one of Many Faces. How can you seek that which you already have? I have not come to bring you pain. I have come to remind you of that which you know. For while you sought the lust for all that the eyes can see, you closed the door to your heart and blocked the path to salvation. And while you seek death as a means to escape, you can't see that your soul is perishing. Now the time has come for you to save it."

It was far worse than the dream. The words scathed deep as the point was made. Old Man Pain knew that what came next was much needed. He left her buried in grief and walked back into the quiet night.

It was the smell of jasmine that woke her the next morning. Her eyes stung from the swell. Perhaps that is why she did not see the ray of light, or perhaps because there was none. But there had to be. It had the same smell of jasmine as the last time. Of that, she was sure. Many Faces turned to the west, but there was no ray. She rubbed her sore eyes and called out to it. "Freedom, if that is you, come and free me."

Suddenly a dark shadow passed over her and an angry voice spoke. "You cannot call me by that name, Many Faces, for you no longer know me. Do you not know what you have done? I have not come to embrace you, for you are not worthy of me yet. You traded the cherished gifts of wisdom, knowledge, and faith for things that burn the heart and scar the soul, but the worst error of your way was that you betrayed the love that was in you, and sold yourself.

"No, Many Faces", the voice continued. "I am afraid I cannot help you, for if I take you with me now, you will be dangerously harmed by the second death. You alone have placed yourself in this bondage, and you alone must set yourself free. The sole purpose of your life is simply to prepare your soul for the next." The voice of the shadow trailed off.

If pain was harsh, death was harsher. If she had known that the consequence of the choice she made back then was going to be like this, then perhaps she would have chosen differently or perhaps not. Many Faces was sorry and hoped that she would be absolved, then she could be free. She sunk back down to the ground, buried her face in the dirt, and cried herself to sleep.

"Many Faces, Many Faces, wake up," the pair of smiling eyes lovingly called. "It's a bright new day. Rise up and claim your strength, for you have been given the eyes of a falcon and the strength of the bear."

There was no doubt about the voice. It was Eyes of Faith. Many Faces jumped to her feet and looked straight up. "Eyes—oh Eyes, you are back! I thought I had lost you forever," she squealed.

"You almost did, Many Faces. Had you not listened to the painful truth that Pain and Death told you, you would have never seen me again. They were the ones who sent for me. They said to tell you that although you have been pardoned, you cannot be freed until the scars on your soul are healed. They also said that you will never be as carefree as you once were, but that if you follow the instructions of your spirit, all of your gifts will slowly come back to you."

The news was too good to be true. She did not deserve it; at least Many Faces did not think so. Not after what she had done. But things would be different now, she determined in her heart. Now she would cherish her gifts, listen to her spirit, cure her soul, and restore her freedom. "And will you still be my guide?" She asked.

"For as long as you follow," Eyes nodded as they turned.

It was not a dream. The moment Many Faces said, "I will, I promise," Eyes of Faith trailed a light, and as it hit the ground, it formed the shape of a door. It reminded her much of the way Freedom first came to her. *Would the door talk to her as well?* she wondered.

"Walk through the door, and don't look back," Eyes of Faith instructed.

Many Faces was not about to question Eyes of Faith, at least not now. She walked through the door, and when she did, it disappeared just like the last time. It was as much of a miracle then as it was now.

Many Faces walked straight into the bright sun and stared at the new land. The first thing she saw was the mountain, then the flowers, then the trees and the small brook that ran between them. The air was fresh and clear, butterflies were dancing, and birds were bathing and singing. In fact, she thought they were singing a welcome back song just for her.

Awe forced Many Faces to smile. She touched her lips and hoped that the new smiles would heal her face. "Where are we?"

"Behind you is the past and ahead of you is your future," Eyes replied.

"Oh, that tells me a lot. All I see is a mountain. Is that where we are going?"

"Yes, Many Faces, but be not dismayed. At the top of this one, the scar tissue on your soul will be dissolved and you will be cured. Consider Mount Splendor and the gift it gave you when you reached the top."

Many Faces thought for a minute. "Yes, I remember now. I learned of the true nature of beauty."

"Good. I am glad you remembered. It tells me you are not quite as lost as I thought you were. Shall we?" Eyes invited as they turned to start the climb.

The ascent was much easier this time. Perhaps it was the hope of her cure, or perhaps there was no other way around it. In either case, it was trouble free. She kept her eyes on Faith, and the climb went swiftly. Then, as Many Faces gripped the last ridge, she heard the distant voice of a man coming from the top. Many Faces gave a final push and thrust herself up. It was without a doubt not Mount

Splendor. In fact, it was but a bare open field. This she did not expect, nor did she expect the small group of men and women that sat together nearby. Eyes of Faith saw the look and turned. "Don't be shy. They are here to help you."

Many Faces relaxed. "So they know, huh?"

"Yes, Many Faces, but that is not the point. The point is the cure. Go ahead, you will be in good hands and I will be near."

As Many Faces turned to walk toward the group, she saw a veiled man wearing a long white robe standing in front. His hair—draped over his shoulders like a cloth—was as cotton white as the beard that reached his chest. His feet were bare, and he possessed a power that commanded silent respect.

"Welcome, Little One of Many Faces," he greeted her.

Many Faces wondered how he knew her name, but she did not ask. His deep and gentle voice calmed her spirit, put her at ease, and gave her peace. Many Faces felt at one with them and quietly sat down next to a small woman.

"Teacher, now that we are one, speak to us on Love," the small woman said to the veiled man.

"There is much to say about love," the white-robed man replied, "as true love has no boundary and withstands the scourge of fire, which brings forth an understanding heart. Understanding is the eye of the soul and love is its light, and it is through love and understanding that the soul awakens from its sleep.

"Love is like the sun. It has no price; it is a gift that is freely given to all of life. Therefore, when it comes to you, receive it joyfully and from it give freely. By doing so, it will grow and strengthen. Hoard it, and it will surely die.

"Little Woman, one should never ask 'Who will love me?' but rather, 'Whom can I love?' You are filled to capacity with an unconditional, powerful love that needs to be shared, and there is no greater love than that which you receive when you touch the heart of another. Like an ocean whose water evaporates to form the clouds that pour forth the rain that fills the rivers, so too is the endless flow of love that resides within you.

"Therefore, do not fear the giving or receiving of love, because fear is not part of the soul. Fear is created by the human mind, and through those thoughts, you bind your spirit, create that which you fear, and call it to you. So let your mind be on love, as perfect love casts out all fear. Love gives birth to compassion. Where there is no compassion, there is no love. Love and compassion are the light of the soul, and like the stars that shine brighter on a moonless night, so too will your love and compassion light up the darkness that surrounds you.

"Love lives to give; that is its food. What does it profit a man if he starves his own love? Does a man cut off his own legs because he has fallen? Nay, if he did, would that not cripple him for life? Why then should mankind cut off that part of his own heart wherein love lies? Does that not also cripple him for life?

"Love needs to give freely; that is its strength. The more it gives, the stronger it grows. True love seeks its own fulfillment, and reaches its own depth of pain at the moment of its separation.

"And should you lose your path, love is the way. Love is brought to you when it has found you open to receive it. And like the path of flowing water, so also is love as it too needs a way by which it can flow freely.

"Thus, if you can say 'to know me is to love me,' then you have accomplished much. It is in the need for love and acceptance that true worth lies.

"And like a sunken treasure in a buried ship, so too is the love within you. You are that ship and you have that treasure; and where your treasure is, there will your heart be also. Therefore, search deep within your heart, for it is through the silver cord that you receive the golden light, and if you have the light, then God is within you. *God and love are one*—as God *is* love."

*How could she have strayed so far?* Many Faces thought. It was no wonder death would not take her. And why did no one ever tell her that the love she once had was God? Now she saw why she needed to be pardoned for the first death. Many Faces then spoke softly saying, "Master, if love is within our hearts, then speak to us on marriage."

The veiled man gazed at her for a time before he spoke. He knew that she gave up her freedom for what she thought would be a richer life. Finally he answered: "Marriage is a bond of two souls by one spirit that is sealed by the flesh. Together, that love brings forth a might that one does not have alone. If the bond is only by the flesh, there is no marriage. But when the spirit bonds your souls, the law that is written on the tablet of your heart will be your vow as that is the law that bonds, but does not bind. If you know that law, you will need no law."

Suddenly an angry voice from the group yelled, "Teacher, how is it that you can stand there and say that the laws are written on the tablet of your heart? I have seen the destruction done to the hearts of those who were bound by it. If the heart bonds, then does not the heart change over time, and would that not then change the laws that you allege are written on the tablet of the heart? Isn't that what creates the devastation that I speak of?"

"Yes!" the group all shouted.

The veiled man was quiet as he listened to the cynical thoughts. He was amazed to see how fast they contaminated those that were pure. "My friend, all of humanity shares this feeling of helplessness. The law is not made for the righteous but for the lawless. The devastation you speak of does not come from the broken promise of love. It comes from the broken promise to keep the law that bound you to the flesh. Be not deceived. Love is not a promise—it does not seek to destroy or possess. It is bound by marriage to share so that your joy may be made complete. Love one another, but do not make it a promise as love is like time—both are invisible and timeless."

Many Faces considered all that the veiled man said, and was left with more questions. "Teacher, if time and love are one, and they are both invisible and timeless, then speak to us on deception."

The veiled man looked deep into her eyes, saw the remnants of a cold, loveless past, and answered, "Be not deceived. Water is neither blue when it is sunny or gray when it is drizzly as it has no color. And what you see is only an illusion of that which you wish to see. Therefore, be not deceived by the appearance of the fullness of the world; it too is an illusion. Is not the wealthiest man you have ever met not the poorest, and the poorest not the richest?

82

"So too are your possessions. They are merely things that have no power to sustain happiness. Examine them closely and you will find that they are they like the wind that blows to and fro. And when they are burned, all that is left—are the ashes.

"Be not deceived. It is only those things that are not visible to the human eye that cannot be burned. One cannot lose what is truly theirs to keep."

"Be not deceived. Happiness is a state of mind that mankind strives to make visible by giving power to those things he can see or touch. Do not the butterflies that fly along the shores of the great sea appear to be free? Yet, can they withstand the winds of a powerful storm? And are not the reeds along the waters of that sea not bound by their roots? Yet they do bend in the winds of a storm. Unlike the butterflies, their roots are planted deep in the living water.

"Many Faces, the apparent freedom of the butterfly is an illusion as it too strives to attain a lasting state of happiness. And if you are to attain it, you must seek it where it lies. Your soul is like the reeds. It is fed by the living spirit, bound by the silver cord, and bends in the winds of a storm."

"Veiled man, do you mean to say that neither happiness nor freedom exist?" Many Faces then asked.

He replied, "Many Faces, as with marriage and time, what mankind has created is but an idea of them in his own mind. Freedom is not being free from constraints as this too is an illusion. Even the flight of the butterfly is constrained by the wind. Freedom is not being free of charge, for we are one with life and have been tasked to care for it. You can be bound and be free, and you can be free and be bound. To conform to the values of others for the sake of freedom is to be bound by them. It is but a hidden desire to be loved for what you are not and is a great injustice, because in doing so, your true self dies. Do not be a slave to freedom as it is not part of the external world. Your spirit cannot be bound by others, nor can it be loved for what it is not. True freedom lies within you and your spirit is free.

"Therefore, love all of life to your fullest extent, and share your knowledge with those who seek. How much more fulfilled would our short journey be if we helped each other along the way? The path that leads to fullness is straight and narrow, while the path that leads to death is crooked and wide; the straight one bright and the crooked one dark, for death is the absence of light and darkness the absence of life.

"Freedom is to forgive one another for a perceived wrongdoing. By doing so you forgive yourself and clear the path to growth, and by not doing so is to be self righteous, which will bind you to it.

"Therefore, live in harmony with all creatures great and small. They are part of one life and we are their keeper. Hence, each time you harm a living creature, you harm a part of your own soul.

"Live not in bitterness and in strife, as those too are enemies of freedom. They will bind your spirit, blind you to the light, and your journey will have been for naught. Thus, live in the quietness of your mind, as it is in the presence of silence that you will hear the gentle instructions as they flow from your mind. And it is in these golden moments that you will enjoy the comfort of your spirit as you gain the precious gift of sight.

"Plant your seed in the path of light, as light overcomes darkness, for the sole purpose of life is but to prepare your soul for the next. Through the progress of your soul you reach divine perfection." Upon uttering these words, the veiled man fell silent.

It was the tone of hostility in the voice that Many Faces heard next, and as she turned, she saw hate coming from the eyes of the woman who sat next to her. Her back was hunched and her shoulders sagged forward, and when she spoke, she growled. "Veiled man, I hate to hear you speak on such illusions. Why do you not speak to us on reality? Hate is not an illusion, and it is much more real than love!"

"Yes," a cynical man yelled, "and what about power? Is it an illusion as well? Even I have seen remnants of the death and destruction done by those who have power; and that was not an illusion! Power is money, money is might, might is rank. Those who have it rule, and they are the ones who decide the fate of those they rule!"

The veiled man looked from one to the other. One was filled with hate and the other was a cynic. He knew that they both were a mask for impotence, but that did not concern him as much as their lack of faith. He would get to that later, however. For now, he would speak to the woman's hate. "Little woman," he said calmly, "there is much to learn about hate, but I only know a little.

"Hate is like an unattended weed that grows amongst the flowers, and as it grows, it consumes all of their beauty. So is the unattended hate that grows in your heart. Like the weed, it too will consume your body and destroy the beauty of your soul.

"Be not deceived. Those who curse you curse themselves, and those who bless you are themselves blessed. We are all a part of one body that is greater than ourselves. Thus, each time you destroy a part of yourself, you destroy a part of the very world you seek to preserve.

"Be not deceived. Hate does not destroy that which you wish it to destroy, as hate is but a symbiotic need for love.

"Beware of the hate that grows amongst you. After it consumes you, you will then become the very thing you hate."

It was good to see the flame of anger go out so quickly. What awed Many Faces was that the hump on the hate-filled woman's back was gone, and a look of peace was now in her eyes. Was it was love that had cured her? Many Faces was about to ask when she heard the veiled man say:

"Young man, along with the power to heal comes the power to kill, and *you* have that power. The remnants of the death and destruction that you spoke of are not of power, but are of greed. And all that the eye can see, it desires to possess, and is but emptiness gone unnoticed.

"My friend," he added, "you can be imprisoned and be free, and you can be free and be imprisoned by your own soul.

"Power is not money as it does not burn. Money is merely a false standard by which those who have amassed it measure the worth of those who have not.

"Power is not might. Might is merely a tool used by those who have physical strength against those who do not.

"Power is not rank, for that—along with those in it—is a mere place in time given to them by their fellowman.

"True power lies within you. Its worth cannot be measured, nor can it be given to you by your fellowman. Thus, while you conform to the whims of the world, you bind your spirit and place it in their hands. A ship without a captain will be lost in the dark of night, and dark does not overcome light. Young man, you are that ship, and your spirit is both the captain and the light that shines in the darkness of your soul.

"Therefore, let not your weakness be for power, but let it be for the sake of love because therein lies your strength. There is no height or depth it cannot reach, no mountain that it cannot cross, and no creature that it cannot touch—for there is no greater power, than the *power of love*.

"And for this, my friend, you must have faith. Faith is like a deep well that is filled with living water, and if that water is not used, does it not then become stale? So too is faith, as faith not used will also become stale.

"My friend, do you not see that the earth is filled with darkness even at high noon? And yet, the blind man sees.

"Faith is like a moonless night that brings forth darkness as a promise of the light to come. Like a ship sailing under a starless night, so too are those who walk in darkness, and even if you are at the helm of your ship, can you calm a storm or the storm tossed waters? Nay, for the conflict is not between men. The conflict is with man and God over the rule of his destiny, and his destiny lies in the hands of his spirit.

"Faith does not know that there will be a tomorrow, but hopes that there is. There is no life in yesterday. Yesterday is but a memory in time. There is no life in tomorrow, for tomorrow is only a hope, and without faith, there is no hope. Even dogs have faith in their masters.

"Faith is the evidence of things not seen, but the hope for them. Therefore, hope for that which is not seen, and know that which is hoped for will come about." The veiled man then went silent.

Many Faces turned to look at the cynic, saw his peace and was jealous. She wanted her face to look like that. Why had she not been healed? She knew that she had lived the lie, bound her spirit, and given up her freedom, but then she followed Eyes of Faith and was pardoned. So, what was she missing?

The veiled man took note of her confusion. He looked deep into her eyes, saw the missing part, and said, "Many Faces, your fellowman is not your enemy, but rather the lust for greed, envy, strife, hate, and fear which are all part of the human heart. They are the powerful forces that lurk in the shadow of the hearts of those who seek to embrace them. And for each embrace you give them, you lose a part of yourself — for each one of them destroys a part of the soul and darkens the beauty of the heart.

"To know your enemy is to know yourself; to face your enemy is to face yourself, and to love your enemy is to love yourself because *you* are the enemy.

"Do not think that you are something when you are not. The greatest man I have ever met was a simple one. What good is it if you are so high above others that you are no earthly good? Can you stop the day from breaking or the night from falling? Can you see the unseen or hear what the spirits say? Can you see what the blind man sees or hear what the deaf man hears? Nay, for we are blinder than the blind man and deafer than the deaf man, and only God can stop the day from breaking forth. Many Faces, to be great, you must put yourself last as a humble spirit and a contrite heart are worthy of honor.

"Therefore, love yourself and then you will love others, and give to them that which you need for yourself. By doing so, your cup will never be empty, and your reward will be great.

"Be not deceived. There are many faces of givers. There are those who have learned to give little and those who learned to give much. There are those who have learned to give expectantly and those who have not. There are those who give for the sake of giving, and those who hide themselves behind the gift they give.

"But this I say to you: In all that you give, do it freely. Our presence here is not to stay or possess, but rather to give and to share. They are bound by love and the giver is but an instrument of God. For this reason, give all that you can while you may still receive the joy of giving as there will come a time when all that you have will be given."

As the veiled man watched the change in Many Faces' eyes, he heard the heart-piercing sound in the voice of the man who cried out, "Teacher, speak to us on pain."

The veiled man turned to him. It hurt to the core of his being to see his pain. Was there a way to soothe it? Perhaps there was. His eyes welled with tears, and his voice broke when he said, "There is much to learn about pain, for the pain of life is greater than the pain of death. Though there is much pain in the giving of birth to the spirit of life, there is much more in being as the pain of birth is equal to that of separation. And just as each man clothes himself each day from his own wardrobe of cloth, so too does each man's spirit clothe itself from its own wardrobe of flesh as we are all one spirit clothed in flesh.

"And like the fullness and emptiness in the ebb and flow of tide on the shore, and like a moonless night that brings forth darkness as a promise of the light to come, so too shall we once again be a seed in the womb of a woman. Death and life are one, life is the seed and death is its fruit, and the fruit must die before it can live again.

"Thus, when your companion is gone, exult for him; by doing so, you honor their freedom. Those who grieve, do so for themselves as it is those who remain captured by the thoughts of their beloved that are stored in the memory of his time.

"If you are to grieve, do so for those who remain. There are those who seek the living and those who seek the dead. There are those who seek to kill the living and strive to put life into those things that are dead. And there are those who in their selfishness cause much pain to others, and those who have lost their way.

"Grieve for those whose love has gone astray as it was never theirs to have. But, above all, grieve for those who have never loved at all for they are living amongst the dead.

"My friend," he continued, "pain brings forth growth and compassion, and builds an understanding heart. There is a time to laugh and a time to cry, and there comes a time when all souls must travel through the desert before they reach the Promised Land.

"Pain is likened to that of the birth of a child. Before our soul gives birth to light, it must first live in the darkness of it. My friend, the barrenness of the desert is but an illusion as it too is filled with life.

"And if you accept that part of your journey, you will wake to the abundance of life. Like the seed of a flower breaks open the ground to bring forth new beauty, so too does pain break open our hearts to bring forth new growth and light. And as the seed that breaks open the ground to bring forth a new weed, so too does pain that comes forth in vain.

"Therefore, if you are to fear, let it not be for the pain of life, but rather let it be for a life without love. For we are only here for the sake of our souls, and if your seed is not planted in fertile ground, it will remain but a dead seed.

"Your soul is that seed, love is the fertile ground, and death is the redemption thereof." Then he was silent.

The familiar sweet smell of jasmine permeated the air around Many Faces and woke her. When had she fallen asleep? She could not remember. The last thing that she remembered was following Eyes of Faith up the mountain. When did she reach the top? And where was the rest of the group? Moreover, where was the veiled man?

Confused and drowsy, Many Faces turned to the west to look for the radiant light and saw the veiled man standing beside her. "Oh. So I was not dreaming," she said.

Without responding, the veiled man drew her close, fixed his eyes on hers and slowly began to lift his veil. In that moment, Many Faces sensed a feeling of warmth—the same warmth that enveloped her being and touched her very soul when she first discovered that she was the gold and love was within her heart.

She looked around, but the veiled man was gone. It was only a mirage. He was she, and it was *her* veil! The small group of men and women she thought she had been with were, in truth, different parts of her own spirit that were finally unveiled. The scar tissue on her soul dissolved, and she was healed.

It was the Dove of Peace, the Eyes of Faith, and Elusive, the Golden Yellow Butterfly of Happiness that accompanied the radiant light. And as they moved forward, the trumpets sounded and they all sang, *"Welcome home, Many Faces, you are now free."* The radiant light of Freedom then fully engulfed her, and Many Faces instantly knew that she had just been born again.

# Epilogue

It is in the presence of silence that you hear the gentle instructions as they quietly flow from your mind, and in these golden moments of solitude that you enjoy the comfort of your spirit as you gain the precious gift of sight.

Printed in the United States
62472LVS00002B/1-99

9 781594 678660